SIMONE ELKELES

LEAVING PARADISE

Woodbury, Minnesota

First Edition
Eighth Printing, 2010

Book design by Steffani Chambers
Cover design by Lisa Novak
Cover illustration © Antonio Mo/Taxi/Getty Images
Editing by Rhiannon Ross

Flux, an imprint of Llewellyn Publications

The Cataloging-in-Publication Data for *Leaving Paradise* is on file at the Library of Congress.
  ISBN-13: 978-0-7387-1018-1
  ISBN-10: 0-7387-1018-0

Flux
Llewellyn Publications
A Division of Llewellyn Worldwide, Ltd.
2143 Wooddale Drive, Dept. 978-0-7387-1018-1
Woodbury, MN 55125-2989, U.S.A.
www.fluxnow.com

Printed in the United States of America

Leaving
Paradise

ALSO BY SIMONE ELKELES

How to Ruin a Summer Vacation
How to Ruin My Teenage Life
How to Ruin Your Boyfriend's Reputation

For Brett
who brightens my day just by looking at him

Acknowledgments

First of all I want to thank my agent, Nadia Cornier, for always believing in my stories and my talent. I also want to thank my editor, Andrew Karre, for his insight and support while I wrote this book, along with Brian Farrey and Rhiannon Ross, two people who deserve medals for putting up with all my questions and changes. Lisa Novak gets special kudos for designing the beautiful cover!

Karen Harris's, Marilyn Weigel's, and Ruth Kaufman's advice has been invaluable while I wrote this book—you ladies ROCK! Other friends who have been incredibly supportive are Lisa Laing, Sara Daniel, Erika Danou-Hasan (hereby officially dubbed The Nice One), Martha Whitehead, Amy Kahn-Randi Sak-Liane Freed-Debbie Feiger-Marianne To-Stacy Leiter-Michelle Movitz (after my surgery you all went above and beyond the call of duty), Nanci Martinez (who has the Spaghetti Spectacular recipe), and the plethora of friends I have in Chicago-North RWA. A special thanks to Heather Davis and my www.booksboysbuzz.com blog friends.

And to Pat McCurdy, whose music always makes me laugh when I'm going through the toughest of days.

Thanks to Dylan Harris for his brilliant wrestling advice and to my cousin Rob Adelman for being such an inspiration.

Derrick Bankston spent hours with me at the Juvenile Justice Complex and his hospitality went beyond my highest expectations. If my kids ever get into trouble, I'm calling you for advice.

And finally to Samantha, Brett, Moshe, and Fran (a.k.a. Mom). We're on this journey together. Whee!

ONE

Caleb

I've been waiting a year for this moment. It's not every day you get a chance to get out of jail. Sure, in the game of Monopoly you just have to roll the dice three times and wait for a double, or pay the fine and be free. But there are no games here at the Illinois Department of Corrections–Juvenile complex; or the DOC as we inmates call it.

Oh, it's not as rough as it sounds. The all male juvenile division is tough, but it's not like the adult DOC. You might ask why I've been locked up for the past year. I was convicted of hitting a girl with my car while driving drunk. It was a hit-and-run accident, too, which actually made the judge in my case royally pissed off. He tacked on an extra three months for that.

"You ready, Caleb?" Jerry, the cell guard, asks.

"Yes, sir." I've been waiting three hundred and ten days for this. Hell, yeah, I'm ready.

I take a deep breath and follow Jerry to the room where the review committee will evaluate me. I've been prepped by the other guys in my cell block. *Sit up straight, look full of remorse, act polite,* and all that stuff. But, to tell you the truth, how much can you trust guys who haven't gotten out themselves?

As Jerry opens the door to the evaluation room, my muscles start to twitch and I'm getting all sweaty beneath my state-issued coveralls, state-issued socks, and yep, even my state-issued briefs. Maybe I'm not so ready for this after all.

"Please sit down, Caleb," orders a woman wearing glasses and a stern look on her face.

I swear the scene is out of a bad movie. Seven people sitting behind six-foot-long tables in front of one lone metal chair.

I sit on the cold, hard metal.

"As you know, we're here to evaluate your ability to leave here and begin your life as a free citizen."

"Yes, ma'am," I say. "I'm ready to leave."

A big guy, who I can tell is going to play "bad cop," puts his hand up. "Whoa, slow down. We have a few questions to ask before we make our decision."

Oh, man. "Sorry."

Big Guy checks my file, flipping page after page. "Tell me about the night of the accident."

The one night in my life I want to erase from history. Taking a deep breath, I say, "I was drinking at a party. I drove home, but lost control of the car. When I realized I hit someone, I freaked and drove back to the party."

"You knew the girl you hit?"

Memories assault me. "Yes, sir. Maggie Armstrong . . . my neighbor." I don't add she was my twin sister's best friend.

"And you didn't get out of the car to see if your neighbor was hurt?"

I shift in my chair. "I guess I wasn't thinking straight."

"You *guess?*" another committee member asks.

"If I could turn back time, I swear I would. I'd change everything."

They question me for another half hour and I spurt out answers. Why I was drinking while underage, why I'd get into a car drunk, why I left the scene of the accident. I don't know if I'm saying the wrong thing or right thing, which puts me on edge. I'm just being me . . . seventeen-year-old Caleb Becker. If they believe me, I stand a chance of getting released early. If they don't . . . well, I'll be eating crappy food for another six months and continue rooming with convicts.

Big Guy looks right at me. "How do we know you won't go on another drinking binge?"

I sit up straight in my chair and direct my attention to each and every one of the committee members. "No offense, but I never want to come back here again. I made a huge mistake, one that's haunted me day and night since I've been here. Just . . . let me go home." For the first time in my life, I'm tempted to grovel.

Instead, I sit back and wait for another question.

"Caleb, please wait outside while we make our decision," the woman with the glasses says.

And it's over. Just like that.

I wait out in the hall. I'm usually not a guy who breaks under pressure, and the past year in jail has definitely given me an invisible piece of armor I wear around me. But waiting for a group of strangers to decide your fate is majorly nerve-wracking. I wipe beads of perspiration off my forehead.

"Don't worry," guard Jerry says. "If you didn't win them over, you might get another chance in a few months."

"Great," I mumble back, not consoled in the least.

Jerry chuckles, the shiny silver handcuffs hanging off his belt clinking with each movement. The dude likes his job too much.

We wait a half hour for someone to come out of the room and give me a sign of what's next. Freedom or more jail time?

I'm tired of being locked in my cell at night.

I'm tired of sleeping on a bunk bed with springs pushing into my back.

And I'm tired of being watched twenty-four hours a day by guards, personnel, cameras, and other inmates.

The lady with the glasses opens the door. "Caleb, we're ready for you."

She isn't smiling. Is that a bad sign? I'm bracing myself

for bad news. I stand up and Jerry pats me on the back. A pity pat? Does he know something I don't? The suspense is freaking me out.

I sit back on the metal chair. All eyes are on me. Big Guy folds his hands on the table and says, "We all agree that your actions last year concerning the accident were reprehensible."

I know that. I *really* know that.

"But we believe that was an isolated incident never to be repeated. You've demonstrated positive leadership qualities with other inmates and worked hard on your jobs here. The review committee has decided to release you and have you finish out your sentence with one hundred and fifty hours of community service."

Does that mean what I think it means? "Release? As in I can leave here?" I ask the Big Guy.

"You'll be meeting with your transition coach tomorrow morning. He'll arrange your community service duties and report your progress to us."

Another member of the committee points a manicured finger at me. "If you screw up, your transition counselor can petition the judge to bring you back here to serve out the rest of your sentence. Do you understand?"

"Yes, sir."

"We don't give breaks to repeaters. Go back home, be a model citizen, finish your community service requirements, and have a good, clean life."

I *get it*. "I will," I say.

When I get back to my cell, the only one here is the new kid. He's twelve and still cries all the time. Maybe he should've thought twice before he buried a knife into the back of the girl who refused to go to the school dance with him.

"You ever gonna stop crying?" I ask the kid.

He's got his face in his pillow; I don't think he hears me. But then I hear a muffled, "I hate this place. I want to go home."

I change into my work boots because I get the pleasure of having to clean the dumpsters today. "Yeah, me too," I say. "But you're stuck here so you might as well suck it up and get with the program."

The kid sits up, sniffles, and wipes his nose with the back of his hand. "How long have you been here?"

"Almost a year."

That sets the kid plunging back into his pillow for more wailing. "I don't want to be locked up for a year," he cries.

Julio, another cell mate, walks into the room. "Seriously, Caleb, if that kid doesn't shut up, I'm gonna kill him. I haven't slept for three nights because of that crybaby."

The wails stop, but then the sniffles start. Which are actually worse than the wailing.

"Julio, give the kid a break," I say.

"You're too soft, Caleb. Gotta toughen these kids up."

"So they can be like you? No offense, man, but you'd scare a serial killer," I say.

One look at Julio and you know he's a tough guy. Tattoos all over his neck, back, and arms. Shaved head. When my mom comes for visits, she acts like his tattoos are contagious.

"So?" Julio says. "They gonna let you outta here?"

I sit on my bed. "Yeah. Tomorrow."

"Lucky sonofabitch. You goin' back to that small town with a funny name? Wha's it called again?"

"Paradise."

"So I'll be stuck here alone with crybaby while you're in Paradise? Ain't that a bitch." He gives the kid a wide-eyed stare. If I didn't know Julio better, I'd be afraid, too.

This sets the kid off again.

Julio chuckles, then says "Well, I'll give you the number to my cousin Rio in Chicago. If you need to hightail it out of Paradise, Rio will hook you up."

"Thanks, man," I say.

Julio shakes his head at the crying kid, says "Later, *amigo*," and leaves the open cell.

I tap the kid on his shoulder. He jerks away, scared.

"I'm not gonna hurt you," I tell him.

He turns to me. "That's what they all say. I heard about what goes on in jails." He scoots his butt towards the wall.

"Don't flatter yourself, kid. You're not my type. I like chicks."

"What about the guy with the tattoos?"

I fight the urge to laugh. "He's hetero, too. Dude, you're in a juvenile facility."

"He said he'll *kill* me."

"He says that because he likes you," I assure him. Julio has a sick sense of humor. "Now get off the bed, stop the crying, and go to group."

Group is group therapy. Where all the inmates sit around and discuss personal shit about their lives.

Tomorrow I'm getting the hell out of this place. No more group. No more cellmates. No more crappy food. No more cleaning dumpsters.

Tomorrow I'm going home.

TWO

Maggie

I think physical therapists like their job a little too much. I mean, why do they always look so happy and smiley as they make you sweat and wince from pain?

Sure enough, Robert, my physical therapist, is waiting for me with a big white-toothed smile in the lobby of the outpatient area of the hospital.

"Hi, Maggie. You ready to work that leg of yours?"

Not really. "I guess so," I say, looking down at the floor.

I know it's Robert's job to try and make me walk better. But there's no use in helping me walk normal because my leg is all messed up inside. The last surgery I had to fix my tibial plateau fracture lasted over seven hours. My orthopedic surgeon jokes with me and calls it a bionic leg.

All I know is that I have more nails and plastic inside me than the average tool box.

When I go to Spain next semester the screeners at the airport are going to have a field day with me. They'll probably ask me to climb inside the x-ray machine to make sure I'm not concealing a weapon inside my knee.

Robert escorts me into the physical therapy room. I have to come here twice a week. Twice a week for almost a year and still people stare at me when I walk.

"Maggie, lie down and put your foot on my shoulder," Robert instructs, getting down to business-as-usual.

Sighing, I lay down on the mat and put my foot on Robert's shoulder. He holds my foot in place and leans forward. "Put pressure on it."

After the accident, all I can do is a little baby push.

"Come on, Maggie. You can do better than that. I hardly feel it."

I put my forearm over my eyes. "It's never going to get better than this."

"Sure it will. Look, you never believed you'd be able to walk again and here you are."

I put more pressure on my foot.

"Thatta girl. Rate your pain level right now from one to ten, ten being excruciating."

"Eight."

"An eight?"

It might even be a nine.

"If you work hard now, the payoff will show later," he says.

I don't answer, but keep the increased pressure on my foot. He leans back and lowers my foot. Phew, that's over.

"Great. Now keep your legs straight and alternate bending them one at a time."

I start with my right leg. The accident didn't mess it up too much and the scars have healed. For the most part.

But when I have to bend my left leg, it feels like a weight is attached to it. I bend it an inch at a time. Just lifting my leg makes me sweat like a long-distance runner. The word *pathetic* pretty much sums up my seventeen-year-old life.

"A little more," Robert says just as I'm about to lower it. "What's your pain level from one to ten?"

Before I can answer a nine, his cell phone rings. And rings. And rings. "Aren't you going to answer it?" I ask.

"Not while I have a client. Keep bending those legs, Maggie."

"Maybe it's important," I say with hope in my voice.

"If it is, they'll leave a message. Dr. Gerrard tells me you'll be leaving us in January," he says as I alternate legs.

"Yep," I say between clenched teeth. "I got a scholarship to go to Spain for a semester. I had to petition for an extension because of the infection."

Robert whistles appreciatively. "Spain, huh? You're a lucky lady."

Lucky? I am *not* lucky. Lucky people don't get hit

by cars and have to go through painful physical therapy. Lucky people don't have divorced parents and a dad they see once a year. Lucky people have friends. Now that I think about it, I'm probably the unluckiest person in the entire universe.

I endure leg torture for another twenty minutes. I'm so ready to leave, but I know it's not over. The last thing Robert does in physical therapy is massage my leg muscles. I pull down my workout pants and sit on the metal table in my shorts.

"Is the redness fading?" Robert asks as he rubs medicated cream on my leg with gloved hands.

"I don't know," I say. "I don't like to look at it." In fact, I'd look anywhere except my scarred left leg. It's ugly, as if a two-year-old drew red lines with a crayon up and down my calf and thigh. But the marks aren't from a crayon. They're from my various surgeries after Caleb Becker hit me while driving drunk.

I try to forget about Caleb, but I can't. He's embedded into my brain like cancer. My nightmares of the accident have stopped, though, thank God. Those lasted for over six months. I hate Caleb. I hate what he did to me and I'm glad he's far away. I try not to think about where he's gone. If I think about it too hard, I'll probably feel guilty. So I don't think about it and trudge through my life ignoring the parts that'll pull me under so far I won't be able to get up.

As Robert studiously massages my leg muscles, I wince.

"It shouldn't hurt when I do this," he says.

"It doesn't." It's just . . . I don't like people touching my scars. I can't even stomach touching them.

Robert examines my leg. "The deep redness will fade eventually. Give it a few more months."

Robert finally announces he's finished. As I put my workout pants back on, he writes something down in my file. His pen moves faster than I can talk.

"What are you writing?" I ask warily.

"Just evaluating your progress. I'm requesting Dr. Gerrard come visit during your therapy next week."

Don't panic, Maggie, I tell myself. "Why?"

"I'd like to switch up your program."

"I don't like the sound of that."

Robert pats me on the back. "Don't worry, Maggie. We just need to come up with a physical therapy plan you can do in Spain without me."

Physical therapy in Spain? Not exactly what I imagined myself doing while overseas. I don't tell this to Robert. Instead, I give him a weak smile.

After my appointment, I head to Auntie Mae's Diner where my mom works. I know it's not glamorous, but she had to get a job when my dad left two years ago. Her boss, Mr. Reynolds, is pretty nice and gave her time off a lot when I was in the hospital. We're not rich, but we have a roof over our heads and Auntie Mae's Diner food in our stomachs.

I sit down at a table and my mom goes in the kitchen

to get dinner for me. I'm about to read a book when I look up and see Danielle, Brianne, and my cousin Sabrina enter the restaurant. God, they look so . . . perfect.

I used to be friends with Danielle and Brianne. Leah Becker and I used to hang out with them all the time. The four of us were on the high school tennis team and inseparable since our first tennis lesson at the Paradise Community Center when we were nine years old. Sabrina was the outsider, the non-athlete. I remember Mom making me ask Sabrina to tag along with my friends when we went out.

The accident turned Paradise upside down. When Caleb hit me, he not only destroyed my leg, he also destroyed my friendship with his twin sister, Leah, and Mom's friendship with Mrs. Becker. There's an invisible fence now between our house and the Beckers' house where there once was an open-door policy.

At first I didn't have time to miss Leah; in the hospital my phone rang constantly. My mom kept busy answering calls and urging me to cut my conversations short so I could concentrate on healing. But as the months passed, the calls dwindled, then finally stopped altogether. Everyone else got on with their life while I recovered at home.

Sabrina used to come over and give me updates on school gossip. Now my cousin is close friends with Brianne and Danielle, which is totally strange because before the accident they didn't give her the time of day.

I've never asked Sabrina about Leah . . . and Sabrina never offers any information. Leah's brother went to jail because of me. I was sure she hated me because of it. We'd literally gone from best friends to strangers overnight.

Every time I think of going back to school on Monday, my stomach starts to do flips. I've been home-schooled by public tutors assigned by the school district almost my entire junior year because of the infection in my leg after my first surgery. Now I'm a senior. I don't know which will be worse; getting out of the house or going to school and facing all the kids there. What if I run into Leah? What should I say?

My cousin and old friends are standing at the hostess stand, waiting to be seated. Okay, so it's times like these I wish Mom didn't work as a waitress. Knowing she wears a pink polyester uniform with buttons that read *ASK ME ABOUT MY DOUBLE DECKERS* doesn't usually bother me. But that, on top of having her serve my former friends, makes me want to hide under the table.

Mom walks out from the back kitchen with my dinner. I watch in agony as she spots Danielle, Brianne, and Sabrina. Her eyes light up. "Hi, girls!" She waves at me to get my attention. "Look Maggie, it's your friends and cousin!"

Brianne and the others give my mom fake smiles. Mom is oblivious.

I give a little half wave and look down at a tiny chip in the corner of the table, hoping my mom will get the hint.

"Why don't you sit with Maggie? She's all alone," I hear Mom say.

Why doesn't she just tell them I'm a loser now, too? Maybe I should get a big "L" for "loser" button and pin it to the front of my shirt.

The girls, including my cousin, just look at each other and shrug. "Sure."

Why pretend to be friends and be all fakey? It's not worth it.

"Hi," I say when Mom leads them to my table and places my favorite dinner in front of me: a French dip, split pea soup, and a side of fries with gravy.

"Mrs. Armstrong, what's your double deckers?" Brianne asks.

The rest of the girls snicker while I sink deeper into my chair.

Mom doesn't flinch and goes right into her spiel. "We have a new selection of double decker sandwiches with turkey and bacon layered with lettuce, tomato, mayonnaise, and our special sauce. We also have new roast beef and cheese double deckers. They all come with two layers of bread in between."

Danielle looks like she's going to be sick. "My arteries are clogging up just hearing about all that cholesterol."

"Forget the cholesterol," Sabrina says. "Two layers of bread? Carb city."

Since when did my cousin become concerned about carbs? I look down at my plate. Carbs and more carbs, cholesterol and more cholesterol.

"I'll have a Diet Coke and a side salad, Mrs. Armstrong," Brianne says.

"Me, too," Sabrina says.

"And me," Danielle chimes in.

"We have thousand island, blue cheese, ranch, low-fat Italian . . ."

"Thousand island for me," Sabrina says. "On the side."

Danielle furrows her waxed brows, thinking it over. "I guess I'll take the low-fat Italian. On the side."

Brianne cocks her head to the side and says, "No dressing."

No dressing? What happened to pigging out on chips and pizza? I've only been away a year and I'm totally lost.

Mom leaves to enter the orders, and I'm left with my salad-eating cousin, ex-friends . . . and my French dip, pea soup, fries and gravy. I was seriously hungry before, but now I can't eat.

Brianne fumbles through her purse and pulls out a small mirror.

"Give me that when you're done," Sabrina says. When my cousin has the mirror, she attempts to check out the back of her head. Which she really can't do with one mirror, but I'm not going to break that news to her.

"What are you doing, Sabrina?" Danielle asks.

"I think I need to get my hair cut before tomorrow."

Danielle laughs. "Girls, stop freaking out. It's a party, not a presidential ball."

"What party?" I ask, then want to die for asking.

Obviously I wasn't invited. I don't want to go, anyway. But now it *looks* like I want to go.

The girls eye each other. They don't want to tell me about the party. Ugh, why did I even ask?

"A back-to-school party," Danielle finally says. "At Brian Newcomb's house."

Wouldn't you know, Mom comes with their Diet Cokes and an extra large piece of pie for me at that exact same moment. "Oh, a party! When? Maggie would LOVE to go to a party, wouldn't you honey?"

Instead of answering, I bite off a huge chunk of the French dip. It saves me from having to answer, but now I feel like I'm going to gag on the gargantuan piece of beef in my mouth.

Brianne looks like she's gonna puke just watching me.

"Uh, you can come if you *want*, Maggie," my cousin says.

It was definitely a pity invite, anyone but a waitress at Auntie Mae's Diner would realize that. I'm not going to the party. I just don't know how I'm going to break it to Mom and let my ex-friends off the hook at the same time.

I take my time chewing.

Before the accident I was a sophomore on the varsity tennis team. But now as a senior I wouldn't even make the freshman squad. Not that I would want to, because then I'd have to wear those short tennis skirts. I'm never wearing a tennis skirt again because I'm never showing anyone my ugly leg scars. Besides, you can't play tennis when you can't even walk straight.

As I swallow the last of the wad of beef, I realize they're all waiting for an answer.

Umm . . .

The hopeful look on my mom's face makes me realize she feels sorry for me. As if I care that I'm not friends with them anymore. Mom cares. She's got to deal with paying for half of the medical bills that the insurance didn't cover. My parents are divorced and I hate feeling like I'm adding to her stress. Guilt, like a big wad of roast beef, settles in my French dip-filled gut.

I want to wince when I hear myself say, "Sure, sounds like fun."

Mom lets out a breath while the girls suck in theirs.

"Can you pick her up?" Mom asks my cousin.

"Sure, Aunt Linda," Sabrina says.

Seriously, I feel like a little kid having my mommy make a playdate for me. Especially when I hear my mom ask, "What time?"

"I guess around eight."

"Grrreat!" Mom says like that tiger in the cereal commercial.

How am I going to get out of this without my mom finding out? There's no way I'm going to a party and have people stare and gawk at me. It's bad enough I'll have to deal with the ridicule in school on Monday.

After Mom brings their side salads and leaves us alone

for two minutes, Brianne flashes me a sly smile. "Do you know the big news?"

News? Um, I haven't exactly been in the gossip loop lately. "That Mr. Meyer wears a toupee?" I heard that about our school principal a while ago.

Brianne laughs. "No, that's totally old news. I'm talking about Caleb Becker being released tomorrow."

What?

Danielle dips her fork in her dressing and stabs a piece of lettuce. "Mrs. Becker called my mom today and told her. Early release. I wonder if they'll let him back in school."

Early release? He was supposed to be away for at least six more months. I had the perfect plan—to leave for Spain before he got back. A deep, sharp pain in my chest jabs me when I take a breath, and my fingers are shaking. I'm having a mini-panic attack, but trying not to let everyone else know.

"Maggie, are you okay?" Sabrina asks as I push the pie away from me.

No. I'm definitely not okay.

THREE

Caleb

A s if having my dad stare at me throughout the entire
drive from St. Charles to Paradise wasn't torture
enough, my mom has been wringing her hands together
since I was discharged from the DOC this afternoon. I
don't even think she's looked in my direction once.

What the hell am I supposed to say? *Stop being nervous, Ma.* Yeah, I'm sure that'll go over well. Her son is
a convicted felon. I just wish she would stop constantly
reminding me of it.

Okay, so it'll take some time. She never excelled at
being the doting mother to begin with.

When we turn down Masey Avenue, Paradise Park is
in front of us. I got my front two teeth knocked out at the

Paradise Park playground when I was five and had my first fist fight on the basketball court there when I was nine. Those were the good old days. I can't believe I'm seventeen and thinking about the good old days.

A block later we reach the familiar two-story brick house with four white pillars flanking the front door. I step out of the car and take a deep breath.

I'm home.

"Well . . ." Dad says as he opens the door. "Welcome to Paradise."

I nod instead of laughing at the most common greeting to visitors in this town. I lurk in the foyer. The decorating hasn't changed in the past year—I can see that right off the bat.

Strangely enough, it doesn't feel like home.

It smells familiar, though. Like apple spice. I haven't smelled this sweet, tangy scent in what seems like forever.

"I'll, uh, be in my room," I tell them, although I say it like I'm asking permission. Why, I have no clue. It used to be my room, it still is my room. So why am I acting like this place is just a pit stop?

I step up the familiar staircase, but this feeling of claustrophobia overcomes me and I start to sweat. I venture farther up the stairs and scan the hallway. My eyes rest on a black vision leaning against the door frame of my sister's room.

Wait.

That black vision is my twin sister, Leah. She's not just

a silhouette of my sister, that's her in the flesh. And she's wearing nothing but black.

Black hair, black makeup. Damn, she even has black painted nails. Goth to the core. A shiver runs up my spine. It's hard to believe this is my sister. She resembles a corpse.

Before I let out another breath, Leah throws herself into my arms. Then these huge sobbing noises come out of her mouth and nose, reminding me of my cellmate.

Even when Judge Farkus eyed me with disgust and told me I was going to be locked up for almost a year for my gross negligence and stupidity for driving drunk, I didn't let out a peep. Man, when they made me strip and did a full cavity search, I was humiliated beyond comprehension. And when Dino Alvarez, a gang member from the south side of Chicago, came up to me during exercise hour and cornered me my second day in the DOC I almost shit my pants. But I never once in all that time cried.

I pat my sister's head, not knowing what else to do. I've hardly had any physical contact in the past year, and craved it when I sat in my cell for over three hundred days and nights. But now, when I'm getting some from my own sister, it feels like the walls are closing in on me.

"I need to lie down for a while," I say, then gently push her away. What I really need is a break from this old/new barrage of family in my life.

As I walk into my room, the dark wood floor beneath my feet creaks, the sound reverberating in my ears.

It's a kid's room, I think to myself. Sports trophies and my Star Wars Anakin Skywalker lightsaber are still on my bookshelf where I left them, and a Paradise High School pennant is nailed above my bed. Hell, even the picture of Kendra in her cheerleading uniform is taped to my head-board as if we're still a couple.

I cut all ties with her when I got arrested. Kendra is a girl used to being pampered by her parents and would be grossed out by the people I've been living with for the past year. I could just imagine her snubbing Dino Alva-rez's girlfriend during weekly visiting hours. The last thing I needed in the DOC was other inmates kicking my ass because I have a girlfriend who wears designer clothes and carries a two-hundred-dollar purse.

Visiting day for me consisted of Mom wringing her hands nervously and staring at me like I was someone else's kid, and Dad rambling on about weather and nothing in particular just to fill in the silence.

Walking to my bedroom closet, I finger all the new clothes Mom must have bought for me. What was she thinking? My t-shirts and jerseys are gone. In their place are geeky, button-down plaid shirts hanging like soldiers. On the shelves, all folded up like in a Gap store, are differ-ent shades of pleated pants.

I pick up a pair and hold them in front of me. They're way too small. When should I break the news to her I'm not the skinny kid who used to live here? I worked out every day for the past year to blow off steam and fend off guys like Alvarez. Muscles don't just weigh more, they change the entire structure of your body.

Sitting at my desk, I look out the window and glance at the Armstrongs' house. My window faces Maggie's bedroom.

Maggie Armstrong.

The girl I was convicted of maiming.

Okay, I know it's unfair. But it's hard not to want to blame her. If it wasn't for her I wouldn't have been locked up. I've thought about Maggie and the events leading up to the accident more times in the past year than I want to admit.

"Caleb, you there?" Dad asks, then knocks.

Gotta love it when people knock. I haven't heard a knock in a year. I open the door and gesture for him to come inside.

My dad walks in and I close the door behind him. He's still got a full head of dark hair and a tailored mustache. He's okay as a dad, but a total wimp when it comes to standing up to my mom.

"Your mom's invited a few of her friends over after dinner." He hesitates, then adds, "For, um, a homecoming party."

A knot on the back of my neck starts to form. I rub it. A homecoming party for a guy who just got out of the slammer? Unbelievable. "Cancel it," I say.

The veins in his neck tense up and start turning a strange shade of purple. "Listen, it's what your mother wants. She's been through a lot this year with you in jail.

Just . . . do what she wants and put on a show for her friends. It'll be easier for everyone if you play along."

"A show?"

"Yeah, plaster a smile on your face and humor the women in her social club. I do it all the time," he says, then leaves the room as quickly as he entered.

It takes a second to register what he just said. Smile? Show? I feel like I've been transported to some Hollywood movie set. But it's not a movie, it's my life.

Taking the lightsaber in my hand, I turn it on. Laser sounds fill the room when I wave the saber like a great Jedi warrior. God, how I used to spend hours dueling imaginary demons with this thing when I was a kid.

Now I've got new demons to fight.

Ones I can't make disappear with a wave of a toy.

FOUR

Maggie

"**M**aggie, look at what I bought for you." My mom stands at my bedroom door in the evening, holding up a pair of pink velour pants and a zippered jacket. "The saleswoman said all the teenagers are wearing these. They're very, very hip."

"Nobody says *hip* anymore."

"Cool?"

I take the outfit from her. It's a Juicy Couture set, totally soft and nothing like my Wal-Mart clothes. "Mom, this must have cost over a hundred dollars. It's very *cool*, but we can't afford it."

"Don't worry about the money," she says, waving my concern away. "I put in some overtime at the diner and have a little extra this month. Besides, school starts Monday and I wanted you to have something hip, cool, whatever. Try it on." Mom does a little excited dance as she waits.

I wanted her to leave for work so I could call Sabrina and tell her I'm not going to the party. "Mom, it's seven thirty. Don't you think Mr. Reynolds will be upset if you're a half hour late?"

She smiles, her excitement hasn't waned. "Sweetie, I'm waiting for Sabrina to pick you up."

My stomach sinks to my knees. "Why?"

"Because it'll make me *so* happy to finally see you go out and have fun."

I feel the pressure building up and entering my lungs.

I dress in the velour outfit, and as soon as my mom sees me she's beaming. "Oh, sweetheart, you look *gorgeous*. Pink goes so well with your olive complexion."

I have to admit, the outfit is gorgeous. But I'm not. Although the pants hide my hideous scars, no amount of money can make an outfit hide the awkward tilt in my stride. After Mom watches me brush my stringy, dull brown hair and lends me makeup to wear, I find myself standing at the door waiting for Sabrina.

"Now, if you have any problems, I wrote down some emergency numbers for you." She hands me her cell and a piece of paper. "The first one is the number to the diner, the second is Aunt Pam's, the third is Dr. Gerrard's emergency line, and the fourth is 911."

Images of Spain race across my mind. She treats me

like my head is as messed up as my knee. "Come on, Mom, 911? It's been ingrained in my head since preschool."

"People forget numbers all the time when they're under stress, Maggie."

I open my Wal-Mart purse and shove the paper inside. "I'll be fine," I assure her, although I'm not so sure myself.

"I know. I just want you to be happy. And safe. But if your leg hurts or you want to come home early, I'll leave work and come get you."

Suddenly it hits me. Why she's giving me the attention she'd give to a newborn baby. "You know Caleb is coming back today, don't you?"

Her deer-in-headlights look doesn't go unnoticed. "Someone *might* have mentioned it at the diner yesterday."

I moan and groan, "Moommm."

"Sweetie, don't think about it. Just look the other way and pretend the Beckers don't exist."

I guess now wouldn't be the best time to talk about how much I miss my ex-best friend who also happens to be "one of those Beckers." A car horn beeps outside. It's Sabrina.

"Go," Mom says. "And call when you get there so I know you're safe, even if you think I'm being overprotective or *uncool*."

I walk out the door, trying to count the days in my head until I leave for Spain. I think it's a hundred and eighteen days, obviously not soon enough. When I get in the front seat of my cousin's car, she says, "Nice outfit."

Sabrina knows well enough that we struggle financially

and my clothes are an extravagant expense we can't afford. Two years ago my dad left on a business trip to Texas. It was supposed to be for four weeks, he was trying to convince a group of investors to move their digital-chip manufacturing facility to Paradise. They rejected his proposal, but they offered him a job traveling around the country as their consultant.

In two years my dad has been back to Paradise three times. Once to ask my mom for a divorce, once to announce he's getting remarried, and the last time was after the accident. He came for one week, then left. He says he's happy, that he wants me to come visit his new home, but he never makes any commitments or sets up any dates. I wasn't even at his second wedding.

"Thanks." I run my fingers over the soft pants one more time.

And that's our entire conversation until Sabrina parks on the street and we walk toward Brian Newcomb's house.

"What's wrong?" Sabrina asks. "You're limping worse than usual. I thought your leg was better."

"It was . . . it is." But a spasm reared its ugly head today.

I hear rock music blaring out of the windows of Brian's house and take a deep breath. There's going to be dancing. Dancing involves moving around and bumping into people. What if I fall? Worse, what if I can't get up and people start laughing?

At the front of the house, I'm ready to hightail it back home and hide out in my bedroom until I leave for Spain. But Sabrina eagerly opens the door before I can retreat.

As we enter the foyer, I'm hypersensitive and aware all eyes are focused on me. A chill runs down my spine. Could it be I have a zit the size of an avocado pit growing on my nose? Is my limp *that* bad? Or is it gossip they crave? Either way, I don't like the attention. I'd just about do anything to remain lost in the background forever.

"Hey, guys, it's Maggie Armstrong back from the dead!" yells a guy on the football team.

"I heard Caleb Becker is back, too," a guy named Ty calls out.

"That's what I hear," I say glibly, not feeling at all glib. I can't hide. Do they know I want to? "It's no biggie." I'm surprised that I'm able to get the words out; my throat is threatening to close up.

"But he almost *killed* you," someone else says. I don't even know who said it; the crowd has become one big blur. I don't even think I could take a deep breath now if I wanted to.

"It was a year ago. I'm over it." Gulp. Being brave is not as easy as it looks. Especially when your heart is racing faster than the beat of the music, which has now faded into the background. Lucky music.

"How can you be? Weren't you in a wheelchair for, like, four months?"

One hundred and twenty-three days to be exact, but who's counting? "I guess."

"People, give her room to breathe." I turn to the voice. It's Kendra. Caleb's old girlfriend. We used to hang in the same circles, but we were never close. She reminds me of a fake, plastic doll. To my surprise she grabs my arm and pulls me out on the back patio. With my limp it's hard to keep up with her without tripping over my own feet, but she doesn't seem to notice. Or care.

"Have you seen him?" she asks in a whisper.

For a second I'm confused. Kendra is popular, someone nobody can ignore. But I'm not really here, am I? Sure, my body is. But my serenity is back at home, in my room where I can hide from the past and reminders of the accident.

Kendra shakes me, and I'm back at the party.

"Did you see him?" she asks. The way she looks at me you'd think her eyes were darts.

"Who?"

She's annoyed, her curly blonde hair bouncing with each movement of her head, emphasizing her mood like exclamation points. "Caleb."

"No."

"But he lives right next door to you," she says almost desperately, those darts narrowing into little slits.

"So?" Okay, so I never did particularly click with Kendra. She knows it, I know it. Not many others know it; we'd been very good at pretending we were on the same page. It feels like a standoff, her challenging me for information she wants and thinks I have. But I don't have it, so I don't even have the satisfaction of holding back information from her.

Brian peeks his head out the screen door. "Kendra, what're you doing out here? Come in and save me from having to play spin-the-bottle."

Kendra looks from me to Brian, then back. "I'm coming," she says, tossing her hair once again with a flick of her head, before entering the house. I'm left alone. Outside.

I'm fine with alone. I'm used to alone. Alone is comfortable for me, it's quiet and doesn't demand I be happy or satisfied or . . . asked any questions. I try not to think about what it was like when I wasn't alone, when I was an integral part of the social scene. When Kendra and I weren't enemies or friends, but hung with the same people. And even if we weren't socially equal, then at least we were on the same social playing field.

Get-togethers wouldn't have been the same without me. Now it's not the same with me.

I sit on a lounge chair by the pool. A few minutes later the party has multiplied and people start congregating and dancing on the patio. I am still alone, but within the crowd.

Brianne is hanging onto Drew Wentworth, Paradise High's varsity quarterback. His hands are all over her as they dance close to a slow song blaring from the second-story window.

Danielle and Sabrina are huddled in a corner, gossiping

and giggling. After a while some guys pull them onto the patio and start dancing with them. The scene reminds me of those California teen reality shows. I stick out like a sore thumb wearing a pink Juicy Couture outfit. I open my purse, glance at the emergency numbers my mom gave me just to make sure they're still there, then close my purse back up. Surely becoming an outcast when you were previously popular isn't considered an emergency, is it?

Kendra and Brian start putting on their own public dance show right on the diving board after changing into bathing suits. Everyone gathers around, chanting for the couple to jump in. Kendra loves the attention, she's used to it. Her family has owned the biggest parcel of land in Paradise for the past two hundred years. Her dad has been the mayor for the past ten years, and her grandfather was the mayor before that. Some girls are born to have it all.

Soon a bunch of other seniors come out of the house wearing bathing suits. Danielle walks over to me. "Did you bring a suit? Sabrina and I are going to change in Brian's room."

If I came out wearing a bathing suit showing all my scars, I'd probably clear the place out. "My doctor says I can't swim yet," I lie.

"Oh, sorry. I didn't know."

"No problem," I say, pulling out the cell.

While Danielle and Sabrina run up the stairs, I hobble out the door and dial the number to my mom's work.

"Auntie Mae's Diner. Can I help you?"

"Hey, Mom, it's me."

"Are you okay?" she asks.

"I'm fine. Having a blast," I say as I limp away from Brian's house and start walking down the street. I don't know where I'm going. Someplace private . . . quiet . . . where I don't have to think about what I'm missing. A place I can close my eyes and focus on my future.

A future without Paradise.

I can imagine the smile on my mom's face as she says, "See . . . and you were worried you wouldn't fit in. Don't you feel silly now?"

"Absolutely." The truth? I feel absolutely silly that I have to lie to my mom.

FIVE

Caleb

I'm keeping a permanent smile on my face at my mom's welcome-home party for me, just like my dad ordered. It's a fake smile, but my mom's friends seem to be buying it.

I think.

My mom has been all over me, laughing and hugging me in public as I play the reformed son. I wonder how long I can keep up this farce before I can't take it anymore. Forget me, how long can *she* keep it up? Dad doesn't even seem to notice her Jekyll and Hyde transformation. Why do appearances matter so much to my parents?

"Caleb has become religious while he's been away," Mom tells Mrs. Gutterman as she grabs my elbow and makes me face the reverend's wife. "Isn't that right, Caleb?" she says.

"I prayed every day," I say, not missing a beat, and knowing it's not only Mrs. Gutterman who's listening. The truth? I prayed every day that I'd survive the juvenile system, come back to Paradise, and make things right again. Mom's declaration that I've become religious is hollow, because we've never discussed what I did while I was in jail. She's never asked, and I've never told her.

Besides, she doesn't want to know the truth. If pretending will heal this family, I'm okay with it. I think it's bullshit, but I'm okay with it.

Mrs. Gutterman is whisked away by someone else, leaving my mom and me standing together.

She leans closer to me. "Button that shirt up more," she whispers.

I look down at my shirt. I only have two buttons unbuttoned. I'm not willing to argue with my mom today. It's not worth it. There's so many things I need to fix, fighting about a damn button would be laughable.

As I'm buttoning up my shirt, I glance at the Goth Girl leaning against the side of the house. I pour a glass of root beer and walk over to my sister. I've tried holding a smile for as long as I can, but my face is starting to hurt from the effort. "Here," I say, handing the drink to her, "your favorite."

She shakes her jet-black hair. "Not anymore."

So now I'm standing here with the drink nobody wants

in my hand. I take a sip. Yuck. "Tastes like licorice. I don't know why you ever liked the stuff in the first place."

"Now I drink water. Plain, old water."

This, coming from the girl who used to spike her lemonade with root beer and refused to eat chicken without smothering it with her own concoction of barbeque sauce, ketchup, mustard, and parmesan cheese. Plain water doesn't fit Leah, whether my little sister wants to admit it or not.

I stand beside her and take in the setting. Paradise isn't a large town, but the word "party" brings people out in droves. "Quite a crowd here tonight."

"Yep. Mom went all out," she says.

"Dad didn't try to stop her."

Leah shrugs, then says, "Why would he? She'd still do it her way in the end." A few minutes pass before I hear Leah's voice again. "Did they make you cut your hair like that?"

I run my hand over the prickly buzz cut. "No."

"It makes you look tough."

Should I tell her what her dyed black hair looks like? I briefly consider it, but quickly realize her blackness goes deeper than her hair. Broaching that subject at a party wouldn't be the best course of action.

Leah shuffles her feet. "Brian is having a party tonight at his house."

"Two parties in Paradise in one night? Boy, things sure have changed."

"More than you realize, Caleb. You gonna make an appearance at Brian's?"

"No way." It's shitty enough I have to be gawked at by a bunch of adults. "Why? You going?"

Leah raises her eyebrows and looks right at me. I get it. She's not going either.

"You should probably keep an eye on Mom," Leah says, biting on one of her black-painted nails.

"Why?"

"Because she just picked up a microphone."

As if on cue, a loud, buzzing sound comes from the porch, then our mom's voice bellows through the yard. "Thank you all for coming," she announces with a flair that would make the Queen of England proud. "And for welcoming my son Caleb back with open arms."

Open arms? My own mother won't lay a hand on me unless it's in a public forum. I can't stomach another word. More than I dread that upcoming meeting with my transition counselor, I dread getting up and speaking into that microphone.

Because what I'm itching to say won't be fake or phony.

I duck out the side gate. As I head down to Paradise Park, I untuck the geeky shirt from my too-tight trousers and unbutton each button until the entire shirt is open.

This is the first time I've felt any freedom since I've been home.

I can go where I want and unbutton my shirt as much as I want. I don't have anybody watching me or looking at me or talking to me or gawking at me. How I wish I could rewind the past year and start over. Life doesn't let you do that. You can't erase the past, but I'm going to try and make other people forget it.

I reach the park and gaze at the familiar, old oak tree I climbed when I was a kid. Drew and I once had a contest who could climb the highest. I won, right before the branch I was on snapped and I fell to the ground. I had a cast on my arm for six weeks after that fall, but I didn't care. I'd won.

I look up, trying to locate that broken branch. Is it still here, evidence of that day long ago? Or has the tree gone through enough seasons to erase the past?

An intake of breath takes me by surprise as I circle the tree. Right in front of me, sitting leaning against the trunk of the old oak, is Maggie Armstrong.

SIX
Maggie

I notice movement beside me and realize I'm not alone.

I snap my head up. There's a guy standing in front of me, one I recognize from my nightmares. He isn't a figment of my imagination, either. It's really him—Caleb Becker in the flesh, looking up as if searching for something important. A big gasping sound automatically escapes from my mouth.

He hears me and quickly focuses on me. He doesn't move, not even when his icy blue eyes connect with mine.

He's grown in the past year. He acted tough back then, but now Caleb has a menacing look about him. His hair is cut short, his shirt is unbuttoned, showing off his muscled chest. That, combined with the tight-fitting pants he's wearing, screams *danger*.

I can't breathe. I'm paralyzed. With anger. With anxiety. With fear.

We're at an impasse, neither of us speaking. Just staring. I don't even think I'm able to blink. I'm frozen in time.

I've been face to face with him many times, but now everything has changed. He doesn't even look like himself, except for his straight nose and confident stance that has been, and I suppose always will be, Caleb Becker.

"This is awkward," he says, breaking the long silence. His voice is deeper and darker than I remember.

This is not just seeing him out of my bedroom window.

We're alone.

And it's dark.

And it's oh, so different.

Needing to go back to the safety of my bedroom, I try to stand. A hot, shooting pain races down the side of my leg and I wince.

I watch in horror and shock as he steps forward and grabs my elbow.

Oh. My. God. I automatically jerk away from his grip. Memories of being stuck in a hospital bed unable to move crash through my mind as I straighten.

"Don't touch me," I say.

He holds his hands up as if I just said "Stick 'em up."

"You don't have to be afraid of me, Maggie."

"Yes . . . yes I do," I say, panicking.

I hear him let out a breath, then he steps back. But he doesn't leave, he just stares at me strangely. "We used to be friends."

"That was a long time ago," I say. "Before you hit me."

"It was an accident. And I paid my debt to society for it."

It's a totally surreal moment, and one I don't want to last longer than it has to. While my insides shake from nervousness, I say, "You may have paid your debt to society, but what about your debt to me?"

After the words leave my lips, I can't believe I've said them. I turn away and limp back home without a backward glance. I don't stop until I open the front door of my house.

When I reach my room, I sit inside my closet and close the door like I used to do when I wanted to block out my parents' fights. All I had to do was close my eyes and put my hands over my ears . . . and hum.

I close my eyes. The image of Caleb, standing in front of me with those intense blue eyes of his, is branded in my brain. Even though he's nowhere near, I can still hear his dark voice. The night of the accident, the pain I've suffered, my whole life changing, it all races back to haunt me.

I start to hum.

SEVEN

Caleb

I'm being tested. Jail. Mom. Leah. Dad. And now Maggie. When I left Mom's ridiculous party, the last thing I needed was to come face to face with Maggie. She looked at me as if I'd run over her again, given half a chance. I only talked to her because . . . because maybe I wanted to prove to her that I'm not the evil monster she obviously thinks I am.

I'm still standing in the park like an idiot. Wind makes the leaves of the trees rustle as if they're talking to each other. I look up at the old oak. In a few months those talking leaves will fall to the ground and die, only to be replaced by new leaves and new gossip.

Right now I feel like an old leaf. I went away, and

deep inside a part of me has died. I vowed I'd come back to Paradise and get that life back, that old life where everything was easy.

I lean against the oak, its trunk so thick nothing but a bulldozer could destroy it. If I could be like the tree instead of an insignificant leaf. I would talk to my mom, to Maggie, to Leah . . . I'd be strong enough to convince them to stop acting like the accident had to change everything.

It was an accident, for heaven's sake.

The kid in jail who stabbed the girl . . . that was no accident. Julio dealing drugs for money . . . that was no accident. I'm not saying driving drunk isn't a crime—it is. And when I pled guilty to the charges, I was ready to take whatever punishment the judge ordered—without regrets.

I was accused of the crime, I did the time. It's over.

There's one glitch: Maggie Armstrong doesn't want to forgive me.

She said I haven't paid my debt to her.

Is there any end to this punishment I've put upon myself?

I won't let Maggie, or my family, make me unfocused. If being stuck in the DOC didn't screw me up, the people in Paradise can't. My sister is going to have to figure out why she thinks being a fuckin' weirdo outcast is better than going back to the way things were before I left. And my mom is going to, somehow, get real and stop acting like she's in a movie. My dad . . . my dad's gonna have to grow some balls one of these days. And Maggie . . .

Maggie's going to have to realize that the accident was just that . . . an accident.

No matter what happens, I'm not leaving Paradise. She might as well get used to me.

They all better get used to me.

EIGHT

Maggie

"How was the party?" Mom asks as she irons her uniform for work the next morning.

"Great."

"Is your leg okay?"

"It's fine." I haven't even thought about my leg this morning; it's the least of my worries. I'm obsessing about Spain. Last night, seeing Caleb reinforced my determination to leave this town. "Did we get the packet from the International Student Exchange Program yet?" The website said the packets would arrive a week ago.

Mom continues ironing. "I haven't seen it. I hope it includes information about wheelchair accessibility. If your leg starts giving you problems, you'll have to get one."

"Mom, please. Do we always have to discuss the *what ifs?*" I head to the refrigerator walking as straight as I can.

"It doesn't hurt to be prepared, Maggie. I won't be there to push you along or help you once you're there."

"I'll be fine, Mom. Stop worrying."

It's sad. One minute Mom is pushing me to go out and do things with my friends like before. In the next breath she's being overprotective, overconcerned and smothering. She contradicts herself all the time. I think it's because she's trying to act as a take-charge father and protective mother all at once. She's getting all confused in the process. She's confusing me, too.

She puts the iron down and gives me a big hug. "I want you to go to Spain. You've been looking forward to it for so long. But I also need to know you're taken care of. It's only because I love you so much, you know that."

"I know," I squeak out. I don't add that her love, like her hugs, can smother a person to death.

NINE

Caleb

I'm playing a one-man game of pool in the basement while my transition coach is yakking to my parents upstairs in the living room. If the situation weren't so invasive, I would find it frickin' hilarious.

My transition coach is Damon Manning, a guy who went through the juvenile justice system just as I did. He's assigned to check up on me and supervise my community service. Lucky me. I have a parole officer with a fancy title.

It's bullshit, but Damon's report will go directly to a judge assigned to my case and the review committee, so I have to play nice. It won't be easy. I've been on edge since I've been home.

I met Damon right before I left the DOC. The guy is a big black man who doesn't take shit from anyone.

My dad sticks his head into the basement as I accidentally sink the eight ball. "Caleb," he calls out. "Mr. Manning is ready for you."

I enter the living room and watch my mom.

"Can I get you anything?" she asks Damon nervously. She's not used to big, black ex-cons in her house, but she's still playing the consummate hostess.

"No, thanks. I'll just be having a little chat with your son, then be on my way."

I sit down in one of the silk-cushioned chairs, but Damon immediately stands.

"Let's go for a walk," Damon says. It's not a suggestion.

I shrug. "Sure. Whatever."

Damon holds onto a manila folder while we walk down Masey Avenue toward the park and end up sitting on a picnic bench.

"How's it goin'?" Damon asks. The guy opens his folder and clicks his pen. Click. Click.

"Fine," I lie.

"Be more specific." Damon makes it sound like an order. Everything the guy says sounds like an order. It just winds my nerves that much tighter.

"About what?"

Click. Click. "Tell me about your family. Seems like you've got a pretty nice home life."

Seems being the operative word. "Listen, my mom is a

robot, my dad's a wimp, and my sister is a fuckin' zombie. I'd say that pretty much sums it up."

I watch Damon close his folder then look straight at me. "Nobody said it would be easy."

"Yeah, well nobody said it was gonna be this fuckin' hard, either."

"Does it make you feel like a big guy to cuss in every sentence that comes out of your mouth?"

"Lay off, man."

"It's my job to stay on you, Caleb. But I can't help if you won't share with me."

I look up at the sky and shake my head. "I don't need your help. My parents and sister . . . they need help more than me. Why don't you treat them like the guinea pig?"

"You've been away for almost a year. Give 'em a break. You act as though they should be apologizing to you instead of the other way around. What did they do wrong, huh? Maybe you should blame yourself once in a while, Caleb. The experience might be eye opening."

"The *truth* would be eye opening," I say back.

Click. Click. "What?"

I shake my head. "Nothing. Just forget it."

Damon opens his folder again. That folder probably tells Damon everything about my life before, during, and after my arrest. I wonder if the time I tee-peed Joe Sanders' house is in there. Or the time I beat up a guy from Fremont High for teasing my sister about her perm gone wrong. I used to be looked up to, the cool rebel. Now I'm a convict. Not cool.

He hands me a few sheets of paper. "You live in a small town, Caleb. Not much in choices for community service jobs, but on your questionnaire you said you had experience in construction and small home improvements."

"I worked construction during summers for my uncle," I tell him.

"Okay, then. You'll be required to check in at The Trusty Nail hardware store on Monday after school at three forty-five sharp. Don't be late. They'll assign you a job site and drop off all supply materials needed. When you're done with a job, get a completion sheet signed. Easy enough?"

"Sure."

"I just have a few more questions. Then you don't have to see my ugly mug for another week." When Damon looks up at me he asks, "Any physical contact?"

"As in sex?"

Damon shrugs. "I don't know, you tell me. Was the old girlfriend waiting on your front stoop when you got home yesterday?"

The urge to laugh gets caught in my throat. "Hardly. My sister hugged me, my dad shook my hand, and I got a few pats on the back from my mom's random friends last night."

"Did you initiate it?"

"No. You're creeping me out, man."

"Caleb, some guys have attachment problems when

they get home. They have a hard time understanding what physical contact is appropriate and what—"

"I touched a girl," I say, interrupting.

Click. "Tell me about it."

I think back to last night, when Maggie tried to stand. The fierce pain she felt was emphasized by her clenched teeth, balled fists, and furrowed eyebrows. Since I've been home, Maggie has been the only person *I've* actually reached out to touch. It hadn't gone well.

"A girl needed help getting up, so I tried to steady her. End of story." Well, sort of.

"Did she thank you?"

I hesitate, then pick up a rock and chuck it all the way to the baseball field on the other side of the park. "She yanked herself out of my grasp. Isn't that what you want to hear?"

"If it's the truth."

I turn and give him a look. He knows I'm not fuckin' with him.

"Maybe you were too rough."

"I was *not* too rough," I say harshly.

"Who was she?"

I reach around and massage the persistent knot on the back of my neck. If I don't answer, Damon'll probably show up tomorrow and every day until I spill the beans. What's the big deal anyway? I glance at the old oak, half expecting to spot Maggie sitting there, her expression wary and angry.

I look over to Damon who's still waiting for an answer.

Then I finally say it. "I touched the girl who I went to jail for maiming."

Click.

TEN

Maggie

"Are you okay?" Sabrina asks.

I'm sitting on the floor in front of my locker at school, figuring out which books I need to bring with me to first period. First days of school are always hard to adjust to after a summer off. I've had a whole year off. I look up at her and say, "Yeah, except I'm dreading Mrs. Glassman's trig class."

"So you're not freaking out?"

"I hear she's tough, but I can—"

"I'm not talking about Glassman, Maggie. I'm talking about Caleb being in school today. Duh!"

I lose the grip on the book I'm holding. "What?"

"He's in Meyer's office."

Wait. One. Minute. "I heard he wasn't coming back to school." Mom told me this morning; she heard it at the diner.

"You obviously heard wrong, 'cause Danielle saw him."

I peek down J Hall.

"I thought you said seeing him was no biggie."

Um . . .

Brianne runs down the hall, heading in my direction. "Did you hear?" she says when she catches her breath.

"She heard," Sabrina says, her hand on her hip. "But she says it's no big deal. The girl has serious denial issues."

Forgetting my locker, I shove the mass of books inside. I'm still sitting on the hard tile floor, but don't trust myself to stand without making a bigger scene.

To make matters worse, now Danielle is walking down the hall with five people flanking her. She's deep in conversation, probably relaying the story of the year.

And it's only the first day of school.

Too bad I didn't get the packets for Spain in the mail yet. I need something positive to focus on today. Because seeing Caleb—again—is a big deal. The biggest. And I can do nothing but sit here and play the unaffected girl. The affected doesn't do so great playing the unaffected. At least when it's me.

"There she is!" Danielle's excitement makes everyone crowd around me. I wish I could snap my fingers and make them all disappear. Or make me disappear. I liked it better when I was invisible.

"So, what's the scoop?" Sabrina asks Danielle.

"Well . . ." Danielle says, pausing on purpose to make sure she has everyone's attention. "My mom is on the school board and I overheard they made Caleb a deal. He has to take junior final exams in all his classes and then he can officially be a senior. If he fails, he'll be held back a year."

"He's a dumb wrestling jock," Brynn Healey chimes in. "He'll never pass."

He's not dumb; I know he's smarter than people think. When we were in elementary school, Caleb got a ribbon for getting the highest GPA in sixth grade one semester. He was proud; you should have seen the huge grin on his face as they handed the ribbon to him.

Caleb got teased by his friends for proudly displaying it on his sports trophy shelf. They started calling him names and accused him of having a secret affair with our three-hundred-pound English teacher, Ms. Bolinsky. After that, Leah told me he gave her the ribbon. Caleb's grades dropped and he never got another ribbon. The relief on his face each time they presented it to someone else was so obvious. Well, obvious to me.

The bell rings and, luckily, the mob starts to disperse.

I just pray Caleb ignores me if we ever come face to face again.

I grab my locker to steady myself and stand. Closing the door, I head toward my first-period class. I'm late, but assume my limp excuse will work.

I catch sight of Leah coming out of the bathroom.

My old best friend walks toward me, not paying attention because she's looking down.

If things were different, I'd ask her why she wears all black clothes. If things were different, I'd ask her how it feels having her brother back.

When she finally does look up and notices I'm in her path, she makes an about-face and scurries away.

ELEVEN

Caleb

The school principal is standing over my desk. The desk has been placed in the man's office so I can take the dreaded exams.

I should never have come back to school. I'd gone to classes in the DOC; it was part of the juvenile inmate program. The tests aren't the problem, either. It's the way Meyer is staring at me like he's never seen an ex-con before. The unnecessary attention is driving me insane.

I focus on the second final exam placed in front of me this morning. It isn't as if I'm acing the tests so far, but I haven't flunked them either.

"You done?" Meyer asks.

I have one more algebra question left, but with the guy

standing over me it's close to impossible to concentrate. Not wanting to fuck it up, I'm doing my best to answer the question correctly.

It takes me five minutes longer than it should, but I'm finally ready for the next exam.

"Go have lunch, Becker," Meyer orders after collecting the test.

Lunch? In the cafeteria with half the student body? No way, man. "I'm not hungry."

"You gotta eat. Feed that brain of yours."

What did he mean by that? *Stop being paranoid*, I tell myself. That's one of the side effects of being jailed. You always analyze people's words and expressions as if they're playing with you. A joke on the ex-con, ha ha.

I stand. Beyond the principal's door are over four hundred students waiting for a glimpse of the guy who went to jail. I rub the knot that just reappeared on the back of my neck.

"Go on," Meyer urges. "You have three more exams so move those feet. Be back here in twenty-five minutes."

I put my sweaty palm on the door handle, twist, and take a deep breath.

Out in the hallway, I don't waste any time and head for the cafeteria. Once inside, I ignore all of the stares. Coffee. I need strong, black coffee. That'll ease my nerves and keep me awake the rest of the afternoon. Scanning the room, I remember there's no coffee available for students. I bet they have a coffee pot in the teachers' lounge, though.

Would they notice if I steal one cup? Or will they call the police and claim I'm a thief in addition to the other labels already tattooed on my back.

I spot my sister sitting alone. She used to sit by Maggie and their other friends, giggling and flirting with my friends.

That's what sucked about having a twin of the opposite sex. It was bad enough when my sister had crushes on my friends and would bug us when they'd hang at my house. She'd slap on the makeup and act all giggly and flirty . . . I still cringe thinking about it. What's worse is when I realized the tide changed and my friends actually wanted to get into my sister's pants. That changed it into a whole new ball game. I spent a lot of time last summer threatening to cut my own friends' balls off. I've always made sure my sister was protected, her reputation as well as her social status.

A year has gone by.

Boy, how things have changed. Nobody even looks in Leah's direction now.

"Hey, sis," I say, straddling the cafeteria bench opposite her.

Leah twirls spaghetti around her fork, the hot lunch special of the day. "I heard about the exams," she says.

I let out a short, cynical laugh. "My brain is already fried and I still got three more to go."

"You think you passed?"

I shrug. "Don't know."

"Rumor has it Morehouse made up a social studies exam you couldn't possibly pass."

Didn't I already pay my debt to society? "Really?"

"Yeah. Caleb, what if you flunk?"

I don't want to think about it, so I ignore her question. When I happen to glance at the entrance to the cafeteria, in walks Kendra. Is she my ex, or did we just take a leave of absence from each other? The answer lies in her reaction to me. She hasn't spotted me yet. Good. I'm not ready to talk to her in front of the whole frickin' school. "I gotta go."

I bolt out the side door of the cafeteria, the one leading to the small gymnasium.

Man, Kendra looked hot. Her hair is cut different than I remember, her shirt a little tighter. How will she react when she sees me? Will she throw herself into my arms or will she play it cool?

I miss her.

I gaze at the wrestling mats piled in the corner of the gym. Kendra used to cheer me on during matches. I remember the last wrestling tournament I competed in. I jumped two weight classes to wrestle the big guy. It was a 1-1 tie before I made my move. His legs were as dense as a python, but I was quicker. I'll never forget his name . . . Vic Medonia.

I wasn't intimidated, although I probably should've been. Vic was last year's state champion. But I won the match. The guy had one word to say to me after the match. *Later.*

I was arrested a week later.

"You're back." Coach Wenner is standing at the door to the gym, eyeing me.

I shove my hands into my jean pockets. "That's what they tell me."

"You gonna wrestle for me this season?"

"No."

"My team could sure use a good one-sixty-five."

"I'm one-eighty now."

The coach whistles in awe. "You sure? You look leaner than I remember."

"I've worked out a lot. Muscle weight."

"Don't tease me like that, Becker."

I laugh. "I'll come to some matches. To watch."

Coach Wenner slaps the wrestling mats. "We'll see. Maybe when the season starts you won't be able to resist."

I check my watch. I better get back and finish those exams. "I gotta get back to Meyer's office."

"If you change your mind about joining the team, you know where to find me."

"Yeah," I say, then walk down the hall.

Back in the office, Meyer plops the next test in front of me.

Damn. I forgot to eat. Now the words on the page are blurred, the knot on the back of my neck is throbbing, and Meyer is staring at me from his desk.

The guy sits there, his eyebrows raised like little French accents over his eyes. "Something wrong?"

I shake my head. "No, sir."

"Then get to work."

Easy for him to say. He doesn't have to take a social studies test the president of the United States wouldn't have a chance in hell of passing.

I should purposely flunk it; that'll show 'em. Then I can skip my last year of high school. There's no way my ma will let me be a junior again. Or will she?

I fill out answers until my pencil wears down and my ass is numb from sitting on the hard metal chair. It's a fifty-fifty chance I've passed Morehouse's stupid test. Only two more of the things to go before I can leave for the day.

Two hours later, I answer the final question on the last test. I almost smile. Almost. My brain is too tired to use any facial muscles. So when Meyer dismisses me, I practically run from his office.

I have to take a bus to the hardware store. Bus number 204 from Hampton will stop a block away from school at three twenty-nine.

My watch says three twenty-seven.

That gives me two minutes to run to the bus. I'm ready to book as fast as I can to catch the thing, because if I don't, Damon'll know I was late.

As soon as the bus is in sight, Brian Newcomb steps in front of me, holding his hand to my chest and stopping me.

"Caleb, buddy, I've been looking all over for you."

Brian and I had been best friends since kindergarten.

We haven't talked for almost a year. I told him not to visit me in jail, so I don't know if we're still buds. But right now isn't the time to find out. Community service sucks, but I have to do it. My freedom depends on it.

"Wha's up, Brian?" I say quickly, then look behind him as the bus pulls away from the stop. Shit.

"You know. Nothing . . . and everything. What up with you?"

"Oh, you know. Getting used to living without bars in my bedroom."

There's one of those really long pauses, where Brian looks like he doesn't know how to respond, before finally saying, "That was a joke, right?"

"Right." Not really.

Brian laughs, but there's something else behind it. Nervousness? What reason does he have to be nervous? The guy knows me better than my own mother.

I narrow my eyes at my friend who'd been my confidante since kindergarten. "Are we cool?" I ask.

There's a slight, almost unnoticeable hesitation. But I see it, and, more importantly, feel it. "Yeah, we're cool," Brian says.

The bus turns the corner. "I gotta go."

"You need a ride? My dad got a new Yukon and gave me his," Brian says, jangling the keys to the car in front of my face.

I'd settle for an old, rusted junker at this point. I murmur a "No, thanks," because I learned in jail not to have expectations or rely on others.

"Listen, I'm sorry I never wrote. There were crazy things going on and you told me not to visit . . ."

"Don't sweat it. It's over, man."

Brian shifts his feet. "I'd still like to talk about it."

"I said it's over. I really got to go," I say, then start walking toward The Trusty Nail.

The last thing I need is my best friend acting stranger than my mom. I have enough to deal with right now, like how Damon is going to spit fire when he hears I was late for my first day of community service.

TWELVE

Maggie

I borrowed a Frommer's book about Spain at the library today. Looking in the mailbox after school, I say a little prayer, hoping the information packet arrived.

There's a letter from the program, not a packet. I rip the envelope open, getting a paper cut as I slide my finger between the folds. I don't care. This is my ticket out, my chance to get away from Caleb and Paradise. Time to forget the accident and get psyched about independence and anonymity.

I unfold the letter quickly, as if it's the Golden Ticket in *Willy Wonka and the Chocolate Factory*. I have a huge smile on my face as I read the letter.

To: Miss Margaret Armstrong
From: International Exchange Student (IES) Program

Dear Miss Armstrong:

It has come to the attention of our IES committee that the scholarship for which you originally applied was an athletic scholarship. Since your records indicate you have not been active on a high school athletic team for the past twelve months, I'm sorry to inform you that your scholarship has been revoked. We are under legal limitations to distribute the athletic scholarships solely to current high school athletes.

You are still welcome to participate in the IES program provided you arrange your own transportation and pay tuition costs which include discounted room and board on the University of Barcelona campus. The cost of tuition for one semester of high school in the IES program is $4,625.

Please remit payment by December 15th to the IES office in order to hold your place in the program. If you have any questions, please don't hesitate to contact me.

Sincerely,
Helena Cortez, President

International Exchange Student program,
University of Barcelona, Spain

When my brain comprehends the words *scholarship revoked*, my smile instantly fades.

"I can't go," I whisper. Mom had to work overtime just to get me a Juicy Couture outfit that cost a hundred dollars. There's no way we can afford over four thousand dollars. I squeeze my eyes shut. *This isn't happening.* Not now. My hands start to shake again. I feel them shivering as I cover my eyes with my palms.

When my mom gets home from work in the evening, I hold the letter out to her.

"Okay, don't panic," she says after reading it. "There must be some way we can manage."

"Mom, it's useless to even think about. We don't have that kind of money."

"My boss might let me work enough overtime. Let's see . . ." She grabs a piece of paper and starts scribbling numbers down.

"Mom, forget it."

"Wait. Sixty hours a week minimum, sometimes seventy . . . and if I work on Thanksgiving and add in my Christmas bonus—"

"Mom!"

She stops writing and looks up at me. "What?"

"Stop writing, stop compensating . . . just stop."

I'm depressed enough as it is without watching her attempt to kill herself to make me happy. I'll figure this out. But it's my problem, not hers.

The phone rings. It's Mr. Reynolds telling my mom

she forgot her paycheck at work. Now she's got to go back and get it. "Come with me, Maggie."

"I don't want to."

"Oh, come on. I saw Irina baking some new pies this afternoon. Pie always cheers you up."

Irina is one of the chefs at the diner. She likes having me try her new pie creations before she offers them on the menu. Irina's pies are one of the reasons I've gained weight this past year.

At the mention of pie, I give in. If there was any time I need pie to cheer me up, this is it.

"The place is crowded tonight," Mom says to Mr. Reynolds when he hands her the forgotten paycheck.

Mr. Reynolds, usually so calm and in control, seems panicked. "It's the men's bowling league," he explains. "They just came in and Yolanda went home sick ten minutes ago."

There's about thirty hungry men milling around the tables, and I only see Tony, a new waiter, looking more frazzled than Mr. Reynolds.

Mom taps her boss on the shoulder. "If you need help, I'm sure Maggie won't mind if I stay for a bit."

Mr. Reynolds smiles. "Really? That would be great."

"No problem."

"You're the best, Linda. I owe you one."

My mom rolls her eyes playfully as she heads behind the counter to wrap an apron around her waist. "You owe me more than one, Lou, but we can discuss it later."

"You got it," he says, then rushes to greet new customers who've just walked in the door.

Mom scurries to the group to help Tony take orders while I follow behind her with a pitcher, filling water glasses.

After I pour the water, Mom tells me to sit down at a booth. I pull out the Frommer's book on Spain from my purse and stare at it longingly. If only we were as rich as Kendra's parents, I'd be able to go to Spain. Even if we were as rich as Caleb and Leah's parents, we'd probably be able to afford it without thinking twice. Their dad is an oral surgeon and has just about every southwest Illinois resident as a patient.

It's times like these I wish my dad and mom never got divorced. I can pretend to forget about the fights, the screaming, the anger lurking around every corner of the house. Mom said they just grew apart while he traveled for work and she stayed home. When he came home on weekends, he wanted to relax while my mom wanted to go out. Eventually Dad stopped coming home on weekends. And Mom stopped caring if he was home.

I'm not sure where Judy (his new wife) fits into the divorce equation. I miss my dad, but he never asks me to come to Texas and visit. I don't want to ask him why he doesn't invite me because, to be completely honest, I don't want to hear he doesn't want me as a part of his new life.

As I'm waiting for my mom, Irina comes out of the

kitchen. "Moggie, Moggie!" she says excitedly in her heavy Russian accent, "I hove a new pie for you."

"Is it with carrots?" I ask, worried. The last time Irina made a carrot pie using an old family recipe of hers, there were chunks of carrots in the middle. I'm happy to say it didn't end up on the menu.

"I promise no weggies. It's a vhite pie viz chocolate cheeps and graham cracker crumbs laced viz caramel. Sounds delicious, no?"

My stomach growls, ready for the rush of sugar. "Bring it out. I need something to cheer me up," I say. "There's a problem with my trip to Spain."

Irina gasps. "Oy, vat hoppened?"

I shrug. "It's a long story."

"I come bring pie right now, da?" Irina says before disappearing into the kitchen. She comes back a few minutes later with a huge slab of pie. I can tell before I taste it this is going to be a best-selling dessert at Auntie Mae's Diner next week.

Before I take the first bite, I say "You're the best, Irina," and dig my fork into the white moistness speckled with graham cracker, caramel, and chocolate chips. She always waits next to me until I swallow the first bite and give her my analysis.

"It's awesome," I say, savoring the moistness of the creamy part and the soft crunch of the chips blended with the smooth caramel and crumbly texture of the graham crackers. "One of your best."

Irina whisks herself back into the kitchen with a flutter.

"I see Irina found you," Mom says as she holds a tray full of double-decker platters. "By the time you finish the pie, I'll be done here and we can go home."

I watch as my mom places the platters expertly in front of the hungry bowlers.

When I take my second forkful, another customer walks in. It's an old lady with grey hair, white pants, and a turquoise jacket. Mr. Reynolds greets her with a kiss on her cheek. "Mom, why didn't you tell me you were coming?" he asks the lady. "Wait, where's Gladys?"

"I fired her yesterday," the lady says. "She was a pain in the you-know-what. Besides, I don't need a caretaker. I made it here without one, didn't I?"

Mr. Reynolds looks worried. "Mom, why can't you get along with anyone I hire to help you? I swear you just fire them to spite me."

The old lady stands up straight with her chin in the air like a three-year-old. "I don't need any help."

"You have a heart condition," Mr. Reynolds says.

She waves her hand in the air, dismissing his concern. "Who says?"

"Your doctor."

"What do doctors know, anyway? They call it practicing medicine because that's all they ever do. Practice. If you'd visit me once in a while, you'd know I'm doing fine."

"I just saw you on Saturday." He huffs, then says, "Are you hungry?"

"What do you have on special this week?"

"Irina will make you anything you want, Mom. Name it."

She narrows her eyes at him. "Corn and a big, juicy steak."

Mr. Reynolds shakes his head and chuckles. "Mom, you have diverticulosis and a heart condition. Try again."

"You're no fun, Lou."

"And you're a barrel of laughs. Just sit down at a table. Wait . . . follow me and you can meet Linda's daughter. You've never met her before."

I look down at the pie, trying not to give away the fact I've been eavesdropping on their conversation.

"Maggie, this is my mother," Mr. Reynolds announces. "Mom, this is Linda's daughter Margaret. Everyone calls her Maggie."

I smile and hold out my hand. "Nice to meet you, Mrs. Reynolds. Are you *the* Auntie Mae?"

The old lady takes my hand and shakes it. "Dearie, Mae was the name of my son's first dog."

No way! I look to Mr. Reynolds for confirmation. He's smiling sheepishly.

"It's true," he whispers. "Shh, it's a secret. If the town finds out I named my restaurant after a dog, this place will be deserted within a week."

I highly doubt that. Auntie Mae's is crowded almost

every night. Besides, there's not another diner within a ten-mile radius.

"I didn't know Linda had a daughter. How old are you, Margaret?" she asks, ignoring the fact that her son told her everyone calls me Maggie.

"Seventeen."

"She just started her senior year of high school, Mom," Mr. Reynolds announces loudly, as if his mother is hard of hearing. "And she's going to Spain in January for school. Why don't you sit with her while she tells you all about it. I'll go in the back and have Irina fix you something to eat."

"Tell her not to make it too healthy," Mrs. Reynolds orders before sitting down on the opposite bench from me. She eyes my plate. "Lou, tell Irina to cut me a generous slice of that pie, too."

I don't think Mr. Reynolds was listening to her last request, or maybe he wanted to let her *think* he wasn't listening.

The old woman places her purse beside her in the booth, then looks at me. She doesn't smile, she doesn't frown. She tilts her head, as if trying to figure out what's inside my thoughts. "Why do you want to leave Paradise so badly?" she asks, almost as if she really can read my mind.

"I just do," I say, hoping she'll leave it at that.

She makes a tsking noise with her tongue. "If you don't want to talk about it, just say so. No sense in beating around the bush."

I had been busy chipping the nail polish off my fingers,

but I stop and look at Mrs. Reynolds. "I don't want to talk about it."

The old lady claps her hands together. "Fine. If you don't want to talk about it, we won't talk about it."

The only thing standing between me and this woman is the pie I have and she wants. And awkward silence. It's not that I'm trying to be rude, I just don't want to put into words how my life has become one disappointment after another. It's almost as if misery is following me and I've been cursed. If I only knew how to break that curse . . .

"I'm sure you have your reasons for not wanting to talk about it. I can't imagine what those reasons are, but you're probably better off being silent and brooding about it rather than talking it out with someone who has nothing better to do than listen."

I shove another forkful of pie in my mouth and focus on the salt shaker at the end of the table.

"You want the salt?" Mrs. Reynolds asks, knowing full well I don't have salt on my mind.

"They revoked my scholarship," I blurt out, then look at the old lady sitting across from me.

She doesn't have a look of pity on her face like I expected. She looks kind of . . . well, angry. "Well, why would they go and do a thing like that?"

I take my time chewing and swallowing, then look up. Mrs. Reynolds has her little hands folded on the top of the table and she's looking intently at me, waiting for my answer.

"I applied for an athletic scholarship, but I'm not on a team anymore so it's been revoked. I can go, but now I'll have to pay tuition we can't afford."

She nods her head, lets out a long breath, then leans back in the booth. "I see. Well, dearie, maybe one day your luck will change."

Yeah, right. All I need is a little magic dust and a fairy godmother. I'm not holding my breath for either of those.

THIRTEEN

Caleb

"Caleb, I hope you passed the tests," my mom calls out from the kitchen.

I'm washing my hands for the third time tonight. I've got paint up to my elbows, compliments of my community service job. The old couple from the senior center signed up to have their kitchen painted a bright pink to match their fake pink roses on their kitchen table. "I tried my best," I say.

"Let's hope your best was good enough."

I dry my hands on a towel, wondering when she'll stop treating me like a stranger. One day I'm going to cut through her plastic exterior. One day soon.

The phone rings. My mom answers, then hands it to me. "It's for you. It's Damon."

I take the phone. "Hey."

"The manager from The Trusty Nail said you were late."

Oh, shit. "I had to stay after school because—"

"I've heard it all, don't waste your breath," he barks out, cutting me off. "Zero tolerance. You sign in for community service on time. Period. You got it?"

"I got it."

"This goes on your record, Caleb. I can petition a judge to have you sent back to the DOC. Keep screwing up and I'll do it . . ."

He's still babbling, but I'm too pissed off to listen.

". . . I told you to be a model citizen and be on time for your job. You let me down. *Don't* let it happen again."

"It wasn't my fault," I argue.

"If I had a dime for every time I heard those words, I'd be a millionaire."

Hardass. "I get it, Damon. Loud and clear."

"Good. I'll check in with you tomorrow," he says, then hangs up.

When I put the phone down, I realize Mom's been listening to my half of the conversation. She's staring at me, but there's an emptiness in her eyes—like she's not all there. "Is everything okay?"

"Yep," I say. Just peachy.

"Good." She grabs her purse off the couch. "I'm off

to the grocery store. I'm going to bake my Spaghetti Spectacular for the Fall Festival Saturday night."

Mom is always volunteering for shit. She loves the attention, I guess. Her Spaghetti Spectacular dish has won the Ladies' Auxiliary best recipe award every year. She's even got the awards neatly stacked on top of the mantle in the living room.

Mom flies out the door in her usual flurry of chaos.

"She's nuts, you know," Leah says from the kitchen doorway.

Today my sister is wearing black jeans with chains dripping from them. The end of one chain is attached to one of her pant legs and the other end is attached to the other pant leg. How can she walk like that?

I watch Mom drive down the driveway as I look out the living room window. "Tell me about it."

"Do you think things will ever get back to normal?" Leah asks, hope filling her voice.

"They'd better." I'm going to spend my days trying, starting right now with my sister. She's about to walk back into the kitchen, but I blurt out, "Do you ever talk to, you know, Maggie?"

She freezes, then shakes her head slowly.

"Not once since the accident?"

She shakes her head again. "I don't want to talk about it, Caleb. Please don't make me talk about it. Not now."

"When, then?" She doesn't answer. "One day we're going to discuss it, Leah. You can't avoid the conversation forever." I put my jacket on, grab a basketball from the garage, and head outside. I avoid even looking at the Armstrong's house as I head for the park in the opposite direction. I need to shoot some baskets to clear my mind.

My screwed-up sister is the one who needs group therapy. I'm the one who was locked up and everyone who stayed home is a frickin' nutcase. Oh, the comic irony.

The next day I'm sitting in the principal's office. Mom and Dad had to come with me to hear whether or not I've passed the tests. God this sucks.

Meyer opens a folder and stares at it. Folders suck, too. Especially ones that have anything having to do with me.

The defense lawyer assigned to my case after the accident had a folder outlining the accident, my arrest, and the history of my life. The warden in the DOC had a folder much the same. It's like I wasn't a guy anymore. I'd been reduced to words written by others about me. Even Damon relies on a damn folder. I could tell them a hell of a lot more than any folder could say.

"While Caleb did surprisingly well in almost all of the exams," Meyer directs his attention to my dad, "he hasn't passed the requirements for social studies."

Gee, that's no surprise considering what Leah said.

Mom's smile loses its brightness for a second. "I'm sure it's a mistake."

I look over at my dad. He glances at me before saying,

"Caleb went through the academic program at the, uh, Department of Corrections."

Meyer puts a hand up. "That may be, Dr. Becker. But he didn't pass social studies or rack up enough credits to be a senior."

I'm going to say what I've been wanting to say all along, to hell with the consequences. "I could just drop out."

Mom frowns. "Caleb, no." Yeah, a real live public reaction!

Dad's eyebrows furrow. "Son, you're not dropping out. I'm sure Mr. Meyer can work something out. Right?"

The guy takes a deep breath and pulls out yet another folder, which seriously makes me want to laugh. He studies the contents while we all wait in silence. "Well, I could put him into a junior level social studies but keep all of his other subjects at the senior level."

"Oh, that's a wonderful idea," Mom shrieks.

Dad nods.

"He'll have to take summer school and graduate late. It's not ideal but—"

"That's fine, isn't it, Caleb?"

Oh, man. Summer school? Why don't they just stick bamboo under my fingernails instead? "Whatever it takes, Dad."

I stare out the window at the cars driving past the school and birds flying to who knows where.

"Caleb, why don't you get a class schedule from my

secretary," the principal says, then checks his watch. "You can catch the last half of third period if you hurry."

Dad and Mom are silent as we exit Meyer's office.

The secretary hands me a piece of paper. "Here's your class schedule."

I walk to senior English. Leave it to old Meyer to make me enter the classroom smack in the middle of class. I wince as I open the door.

I can almost hear an announcer's voice in my head. *Yes, ladies and gentleman, the main attraction . . . straight from juvenile jail . . . Caleb Becker!* I feel sixty eyes on me, burning into my skull as I walk up to the teacher, Mr. Edelsen. "Can I help you?" he asks.

"I'm in this class."

Silence.

Eyes.

Muscles tightening.

"Well, have a seat then."

I walk to the back of the class and pick a seat next to Drew Rudolph. We used to hang out. You know . . . before.

After class I have lunch. I pay for an apple and Coke from money my parents gave me this morning. As I walk through the lunchroom, I hold my head high. Let them talk about the ex-con all they want. Facing these kids is nothing compared to the guys at the DOC.

When I turn the corner, I bump into Kendra. It's the first time we've been this close since my arrest.

"Hi, Caleb," she says with a teasing lilt to her voice. "Drew told me he saw you in English class."

I nod.

"Remember when we had English together?"

Boy, do I. We used to take bathroom breaks at the same time and meet in some deserted hallway to make out and feel each other up. "I remember."

She smiles at me with her bright teeth and killer full lips. I could have kissed those lips forever. I still can.

"Well, I guess I'll catch you later," she says.

"Later," I say, watching her butt sway as she walks away.

———

After school, for community service, I fixed an old lady's fence and hung up her light fixture.

Before I got convicted I'd come home to find at least ten messages from Kendra, begging me to call. But this time I got home and the answering machine only had one message . . . from Damon.

I called him back. Our conversation went like this.

"Caleb?"

"Yeah?"

"Good job today. On time and everything."

"Thanks."

"Keep it up. I'll call in two days."

Woo hoo! He'll leave me alone for a whopping two days.

My dad is working late tonight so it's only me, my mom, and Leah. Leah is pushing her food around on her plate, not really eating. Mom is too busy yakking to her friends on the phone. I don't think she even realizes Leah and I are sitting at the table with her. I'm thankful when everyone in my house is sleeping. It's the only time it resembles the old days.

At night I'm lying in my bed, staring at the clock like I've been doing for the past two hours. Three o'clock in the morning. I can't sleep. Too many thoughts running through my useless head. Maybe I need an uncomfortable and overly used mattress like I had in the DOC in order to get a full night of sleep.

Throwing the covers back, I stand up and pace my bedroom. The picture of Kendra on my headboard is staring back at me, her smile a secret promise between the two of us. I snatch the cordless phone from the living room and take it back to my bedroom.

I dial Kendra's number, her private line that only rings in her bedroom, but I hang up before it rings. What if she's dating someone else and doesn't want to talk to me? I sure as hell don't want to be running after her if she's hanging with another guy.

I look out the window, gauging how long it'll be until the sun comes creeping up. In the DOC, there were always guys who couldn't sleep. You could see them across the way sitting in their bunks, or you could hear them tossing and turning. The new guys and youngest kids had the hardest time. They'd be crying silently, the only indication being a random sniffle or shoulders slumped over and shaking. Even though some of them were just twelve or thirteen, they tried to act like men.

But they were, in the end, just boys.

I notice a light turn on in Maggie's bedroom, the glow outlining the curtains covering her window. I have computer class with her, but usually I sit in the back while she takes a seat in the front row. I keep my head down because the kids in class are analyzing my every move. When the bell rings, Maggie is the first one out . . . sometimes I think she's out of there before the bell even rings. Does she think she's the only one affected by the accident?

FOURTEEN

Maggie

I can't sleep after my nightmares and have to turn my light on to stay awake. At least this time I didn't wake Mom up screaming.

This nightmare was different. Kendra Greene drove the car, not Caleb. In all my other nightmares, it's Caleb at the wheel of the car that hit me.

I guess it's because I saw Kendra talking to Caleb in the cafeteria yesterday. He didn't see me because I sit right next to the doors so I can leave as soon as I've finished eating.

The cafeteria is a strange place. The populars can be spotted right away. They're loud and laugh a lot. The regular people sit in their own cliques, totally separate from the popular lunch tables.

I used to be a popular. Most athletes in Paradise are populars. But now I'm a loner who doesn't even mingle with the regulars, not even the lowest ones.

Loners sit by themselves, scattered throughout the lunchroom. They eat alone, then make their hasty exits.

I never knew where the loners went to, they just disappeared during lunch hour. But now that I am a loner I know that secret place.

The school library. It's the mysterious place you can go to and not be seen.

Caleb isn't afraid of attention. He walked right into the cafeteria yesterday, his head held high as if he was Mr. Meyer himself. Then he went right up to Kendra Greene and said something to make her smile. I swear everyone in the room was silent, watching them reunite. Does he know Brian and Kendra are a couple? The way Caleb stared at her butt when she walked away from him makes me think he's oblivious to what's been going on since he was in jail. Some things haven't changed.

I pull back my window curtains and stare out at Caleb's window. It's a little past three a.m. He's probably sleeping like a baby without a care in the world.

But he's not. His light is on and I see his silhouette pacing his room.

I let the curtains fall back to cover the window, turn the light off, and hurry back to bed. I can't fall into old habits, not now after everything that's happened.

The reality is I had a crush on Caleb since first grade.

He used to tease Leah and me as we played with our Barbie dolls and dressed up in costumes. But when we needed a boy to play a part in one of our shows, we could always coerce him into acting the part. And if we made up a ballet show, we could count on him to be an audience member as we jeté'd and plié'd our hearts out in front of him.

But the time I fell head over heels in love with Caleb Becker was in sixth grade, when he took the blame after I broke his mom's ceramic statue of an owl that had been given to her great-great-grandmother from some former U.S. president.

Leah was upstairs getting ready and I was waiting for her in their living room. We were going to play tennis at the park. Caleb surprised me by flying down the stairs with a Star Wars lightsaber in his hand, waving it around. I laughed and put up my racquet as a weapon, challenging him. He came at me with the saber, and I swung my racquet to ward off his attack. I counted on whacking his saber, not the ceramic owl on his mom's credenza.

His mother heard the crash and came running. Caleb said it was his fault, that he was playing around with the saber. He never named me as the one who broke the statue; he didn't even name me as an accomplice. I was too scared at the time to tell the truth, even when I knew he got grounded for a whole month. Without even realizing it, he became my hero.

After that, I used to watch Caleb through my window when he played catch with his friends or had Boy Scout meetings in his backyard. When we were in seventh grade he started mowing the lawn while listening to music. I could hardly concentrate on my homework while I watched him weave back and forth across the lawn with the mower, his muscles bunching through his t-shirt as he gathered grass clippings and shoved them into garbage bags.

Sometimes he'd catch me looking at him and wave. Sometimes I tentatively waved back, but then I'd close my curtains and keep them closed for a week so he'd never know how I really felt about him. Other times I'd pretend I didn't see him, although I suppose he knew I'd been spying.

Caleb never let on that he liked me more than a friend. That was okay by me. I just kept up hope that one day he'd see me as a girl and not his twin sister's pesky friend.

He had girlfriends over the years, but was never serious about any of them.

Until Kendra.

They started dating in the beginning of our freshman year. Kendra hung out at his house every day after school; they were inseparable from the start. Every time I happened to glance out my window and spot them in an intimate embrace, my hopeful heart crumbled little by little.

That was also about the time my dad left. So here I was, desperately waiting for my dad and Caleb to love me as much as I loved them.

What could I do to make the ones I loved love me back? The only thing I was good at was tennis. So I practiced and played and challenged myself every day during the summer between our freshman and sophomore year. Surely, once Caleb saw I was the only sophomore on the varsity squad, he'd notice me.

And I sent my dad articles from the local paper about my success, never forgetting to add the tennis coach's prediction that I'd make it to the Illinois state championship in October.

That season my dad never saw me play.

That season was also when Caleb lost his virginity to Kendra.

Once, just once, I saw them having sex one night under a blanket in his backyard. I never told anyone, although I could have sworn Caleb looked up at my window and knew I'd been watching.

He never said anything to me about it. And I never told Leah. She'd be grossed out anyway. In fact, after that I felt so embarrassed I stopped watching Caleb.

I keep going over the night of the accident in my head. The conversation I had with Caleb before the accident and the stories I heard about afterward.

He was obviously drunk; the policemen who arrested him gave him an alcohol test immediately after he admitted to hitting me with his car. But was he so drunk he didn't know what he was doing?

So what if he hated what I told him that night, it was the truth. His girlfriend was cheating on him.

"You're lying," he'd said that night.

I was determined not to let him get away from me before

I told him. *"I'm not, Caleb. I swear I saw her with another guy."* I didn't add that the other guy was his best friend.

He grabbed my shoulders so hard I winced. Caleb had never laid a hand on me before. His rough touch made tears roll down my face.

"I love you," I'd told him. *"I've always loved you."* I'd let my fear of the truth and my love for Caleb all come out that night. *"Open your eyes, Caleb. Kendra is playing you for a fool."*

He took his hands off me like I was on fire and he was getting burned. Then he said something I'll never forget. *"You don't get it, Maggie, do you? You and me will never happen. Now stop spreading lies about my girlfriend before you get hurt."*

That warning has echoed in my head from that day until now. The logical part of me knows it was an accident. Of course he didn't mean to lose control of his car. But in the dark recesses of my mind there's this little nagging doubt that creeps up every once in a while.

I finally fall asleep, but it's not a restful slumber because my dreams are haunted by the fact that I won't be able to escape Paradise and go somewhere far away—where the past can't catch up with me.

The next day after school I get off the bus and come home to a message on our answering machine from Mrs. Reynolds—the old lady I met yesterday. She left her number and told me to call her as soon as I got home. When

I call her back, she says she wants to interview me for an after-school job . . . as her companion.

"Are you sure?" I ask.

"I can strike a deal with you so you can go to Spain," she says, totally tempting me. "Can you come to my house in Hampton so we can talk?"

As fast as my limpy legs can carry me I'm on a bus heading to Hampton. It's not far, just a fifteen minute bus ride from Paradise. The whole time I'm thinking of the deal Mrs. Reynolds wants to offer me. What does a companion do? Play checkers and listen to her talk about the old days?

It can't be that hard. I can do it, even with a bad leg. Visions of making the old lady tea sandwiches and lemonade while we sit and talk float in my head.

Leah and I used to talk—for hours on end about nothing and everything. I know talking with an old lady won't be the same as talking to an old best friend, but I think it could be cool.

I ring the doorbell to Mrs. Reynolds' house and she greets me with a smile. "Come in, Margaret."

I sit primly on her expensive, cream-colored sofa, trying to make a good impression. *Maggie, forget about the past and focus on the future,* I tell myself.

Mrs. Reynolds has bright, alert, green eyes that defy her old age, and an attitude that rivals the senior girls on the pompom squad. "Would you mind working for a crabby old lady like me, Margaret, if at the end you'd be able to take that trip to Spain?"

"Besides needing the money for studying abroad next semester," I say, holding my hands in my lap and trying not to fidget, "I believe one can learn a lot from people with life experience."

Did I just hear Mrs. Reynolds snort? "Don't you mean 'old people'?" she retorts.

I bite the inside of my mouth. "Um, what I meant was, um . . ."

"Take it from someone with *life experience*. Don't pussyfoot around, it only wastes time. Can you cook?"

Does macaroni and cheese count as cooking? "Yes."

"Play gin?"

"Yes."

"Do you talk too much?"

Her question throws me off guard. "Excuse me?"

"You know, do you just talk to hear your voice, or do you keep quiet until you have something interesting to say?"

"The latter," I answer.

"Good. I don't like senseless chatter."

"Me, either."

So much for not *pussyfooting* around.

"I'll expect you here from three thirty to seven o'clock on weekdays, a few hours on weekends. I can give you an hour break so you can do homework."

"Does that mean I'm hired?" I ask.

"It seems so. I'll give you fifteen hundred dollars a month, enough to pay for that tuition you need. You can start after school on Monday."

Wow. Way more than I'd make if I worked anywhere else. "It's too much," I admit. "You could probably get someone for a lot less money."

"Probably. But you want to go to Spain, don't you?"

"Of course, but . . ."

"No buts. Buts can be categorized as senseless chatter."

I want to kiss and hug the woman and thank her a hundred times. But I don't think she's the kissing and hugging type. And if I thank her a hundred times, I think she'd have an aneurysm from the amount of senseless chatter.

Mrs. Reynolds stands, using her cane to steady herself. Which reminds me to add, "I have a limp."

Instead of asking me about it, the woman just says, "So do I. So do most of my friends. At least the ones who aren't dead. As long as you don't complain about yours, I won't complain about mine."

And that, if you can believe it, is the end of my interview.

FIFTEEN

Caleb

"Yo, Caleb, come sit with us," Brian yells from the middle of the cafeteria.

I had planned on grabbing a sandwich and sitting next to my sister. Today she's wearing jet-black lipstick to match her black, faded jeans. Mom didn't even flinch when Leah walked down the stairs this morning. I shuddered at the sight. Whoever made up that black lip stuff has got some serious issues.

I'm standing next to her, contemplating what to do. She doesn't look up from reading a book and says, "Go sit with Brian. I don't care."

"Leah, come with me."

She looks up, black lipstick and all. "Do I look like I want to sit with them?"

That's it, I can't stand it anymore. I lean my hands on the cafeteria lunch table and say, "You might want to freak me out with all this black crap, but I'm not buying it. Now why don't you wipe that shit off your lips and cut the death act already. It's wearing thin on my nerves."

Instead of being grateful I'm being brutally honest, she abruptly picks up her books and runs out of the cafeteria.

What the hell am I supposed to do now?

Brian is still waving me over, but I hesitate.

It's not that I don't want to sit with my old friends; I just don't feel like being bombarded with questions about jail. Because these guys wouldn't last one day in the DOC and they'd probably think I was lying if I told them what really goes down in there.

Don't think for one minute that anyone is immune to being convicted. Man, there's so many guys of all different races and religions and colors and sizes. Jews and Christians, Muslims and Catholics. Rich kids who thought they were above the law and dirt-poor kids who didn't know any better.

It's a whole different ball game when you're on the inside, with an unspoken inmate hierarchy and rules. Some stuff you can figure out right off the bat and some things you have to learn the hard way.

Accidents happen at the DOC, and some of them are intentional. Gangs are rampant, even in the juvenile jail.

When there's an altercation between two rivals, you better get the hell out of the way.

Warden Miller has this thing about greeting a new inmate on their first day at the DOC. He thinks it eases the new kid's mind knowing his expectations, but all it does is scare the crap out of them. Unless, of course, they're repeaters. Miller is on a first-name basis with a lot of repeaters. They get a very different version of the welcome speech.

His first-timer speech goes something like this: *"My name is Scott Miller. Welcome to my house. You'll get up at five forty-five every morning and go to the showers. You get five minutes, no more, to wash up. You'll get three squares a day and you'll attend classes for eight hours. We'll get along just fine as long as you respect the rules in my house. If you don't . . . well, then you and I will have ourselves a problem. Ask anyone around, they'll tell you that you don't want a problem with me. My problems get twenty-three hours straight cell time. Any questions?"*

Warden Miller doesn't explain the absence of toilet paper in the cells; that's one of those things you have to find out the hard way. It's when you're sitting on the can and need to wipe. The call button to borrow a roll is on the other side of the cell, nowhere near the seat you're crapping in.

I head over to Brian and the guys, ready to distract them from talk about jail. "Wha's up, guys? Where are all the girls?" I ask.

Drew is sitting across from me and rolls his eyes.

"Practicing for cheerleader tryouts. Don't get me wrong, I love when the chicks jump up and down for me. I just don't know how it could be all that difficult that they'd need to practice for three weeks straight."

"Brianne and Danielle are going out for cheerleading instead of tennis?" I ask. Brianne and Danielle were die-hard tennis fanatics.

"It's because of Sabrina," Tristan says. "She doesn't have enough hand-eye coordination to be a tennis player, so she's convinced Brianne and Danielle to try out for the Pantherettes."

Maybe I've been gone too long. Or maybe I didn't hear correctly. "What's a Pantherette?"

"Caleb, you got to get up to speed, man." Brian is trying to control his amusement as he says, "Pantherettes are the cheerleaders for the wrestling team. Get it . . . Paradise Panthers . . . Panther*ettes.*"

Huh? "Wrestling cheerleaders?"

Drew nods. "Pantherettes, dude. Gotta love 'em. Lots of schools have wrestling cheerleaders, so last year we got 'em, too."

"You wrestling this year, Becker?" Tristan chimes in. "It might be Wenner's last year coachin'. He's got a kid due in the summer, and I think he wants to keep his Saturdays open to stay home with the brat."

"I can't," I say. "I've got to work after school." I intentionally leave out the part that work is actually community service and if I ditch it, I may have to go back to jail.

Brian takes a bite of his sandwich and says with a full mouth, "We need you, or we'll suck like last year."

Tristan and Drew nod their heads, agreeing with Brian. Nothing like peer pressure to make one give in. But the truth is I missed these guys. "Okay, listen," I say. "If there's a match I can make, I'll compete."

Brian holds up a hand for me to give him a high-five. "That's what I'm talkin' 'bout."

I slap his hand. "You're seriously pathetic if you think I can single-handedly make a difference."

Drew shakes his curly-haired head. "You pinned *Vic Medonia*, Caleb. The guy is huge and a legend. Remember when you kicked his ass, getting that five point throwdown ten seconds before the round ended?"

"Drew, please," Tristan says. "Don't disrespect CB here. It was four minutes when he did the throw-down."

"Whatever, Tristan," Drew says, "I forgot you know everything."

Tristan crosses his arms in front of his chest. "Damn straight."

I take a bite of my sandwich while Tristan and Drew are at each other's throats. It's just like old times, except Kendra's not here . . . and my sister refuses to join the land of the living.

Before that thought leaves my head, the girls minus my sister strut into the cafeteria. Sabrina, Danielle, and Brianne come in first, followed by Kendra and her best friend Hannah.

"How'd practice go?" Tristan asks Brianne.

Brianne reaches out and touches his shoulder. "That is so sweet that you care," she says.

Drew coughs. "Why don't you guys do a cheer for us?"

"Right here in the cafeteria?"

"Why not?"

Kendra winks privately at me, then says, "Sure, let's do it, girls."

Kendra stands up front while Brianne, Sabrina, Danielle, and Hannah settle into a pattern behind her. Kendra gets her hands up as if she's about to clap and says, "Ready?"

The other girls respond, "O-kay," then they all start clapping and jumping and chanting:

> *Takedown, tilt 'em,*
> *Or go for the pin!*
> *Stay off the bottom,*
> *And get that win!*
> *You gotta ride 'em, roll 'em, get that pin!*
> *Come on Panthers, leeeeettt's win!*

The girls end their overly energetic cheer on a jump/kick combination.

Drew stands up and claps. "That was *in*-credible! Can you do that end part again where you bounce up and down and talk about riding them?"

"Shut up, Drew," Kendra says.

He holds up his hands and shrugs. "What? I was just admiring the cheer."

"Please," Danielle says as she sits down next to Brian and gives Drew a disgusted look. "You were admiring something, all right. Our chests."

"That, too," Drew admits. "I'm a teenage guy with raging hormones, what do you expect? I bet Caleb admired them, too, 'cause he hasn't seen any in almost a year. Isn't that right, CB?"

I should have known it was just a matter of time before my jail time got thrown in my face. Great, now everyone is looking at me, waiting to hear the ex-con's response. Including Kendra. I stand up and walk out of the cafeteria. I don't want to deal with this crap right now.

"I was just kidding, Caleb. Come back here!" Drew yells.

Every week in the DOC we had rage-intervention classes. They stressed avoiding confrontation, teaching us instead to release anger in other, non-violent ways. Since punching Drew in his mouth that runs like diarrhea isn't an option, I head to the school workout room.

I walk right up to the punching bag and whack it until there's a permanent dent in the side. I don't even care that my knuckles are bleeding.

"Caleb, take it easy on that thing."

It's Coach Wenner, standing near the free weights with a cup of coffee in his hand. He's wearing a golf shirt with *Panther Wrestling* embroidered on the front.

I stop punching the bag and stuff my hands in my pockets to hide my bleeding knuckles. "They tell me this is your last year coaching."

"Yep. I'll be teaching drivers' ed as well as gym classes come next fall."

I shake my head in disbelief. "Drivers' ed?" The guy lives and breathes wrestling.

"The wife doesn't want me to be away on the weekends after the baby is born. Above all else, you got to do what you think is best for your family. Right?"

"I guess."

Wenner takes a sip of the drink and leans against the wall. "You know, what happened last year shocked the hell out of me. I would have bet my right arm a kid like you wouldn't leave the scene of an accident."

"Lucky for you, you didn't make that bet," I counter.

"Uh huh," Wenner says, then adds, "go to the nurse and get those knuckles wrapped," and casually walks out of the room.

SIXTEEN

Maggie

It took Caleb a week to slide right back into his life without a hitch. I left the cafeteria this afternoon when the popular girls did a cheer right in front of him. I could have sworn he thought the cheer was just for him.

As if that wasn't bad enough, I heard Tristan Norris say in earth science that Caleb is going out for wrestling this year.

Not only did I lose Leah as a friend and everyone else thinks I'm a walking freak, I have no hope of joining the tennis team or playing sports ever again.

I'm chastising myself for comparing myself to Caleb as I ride the bus to Hampton for my first day working for Mrs. Reynolds. I just wish it was easier for me . . . or less easy for him. I realize I'm bitter, but I can't help it. I've been through such pain and agony the past year, and going back to school has only emphasized what an outcast I've become.

I reach Mrs. Reynolds' house and ring the doorbell. She doesn't answer. I keep ringing, hoping nothing bad has happened to her. Just my luck she decided to fire me before I even started the job.

Placing my book bag on the ground, I head to the back of the house.

Mrs. Reynolds is sitting on the porch swing. Her head is slumped over, but her chest is rising and falling with each breath. Okay, the woman is sleeping. Phew. Balancing in her hand is a glass of lemonade.

This job is going to be a piece of cake. I feel ashamed for taking so much money from Mrs. Reynolds for doing nothing.

I tiptoe toward the swing. I have to take the glass out of Mrs. Reynolds' hand before it spills all over or, worse yet, shatters when her grip loosens and the glass hits the ground.

Slowly, silently, I reach out and slip the glass out of her hand.

"What do you think you're doing?"

The old lady's voice startles me and I jump back. Mrs. Reynolds has one eye open like that guy from the cartoon monster movie. "I, uh, thought you were napping."

"Do I look like I'm napping?"

"Right now you don't."

Mrs. Reynolds sits up straight, her grey hair perfectly styled on top of her head. "Enough chatter. We have lots of work to do today."

"Do you want me to refill your lemonade? Make you a snack?" *Fluff your pillows?*

"Nope. You see those bags over there?" Mrs. Reynolds says, her crooked finger pointing to the side of the yard.

About ten huge paper bags are lined up in the grass. They're all labeled with strange names: Apricot Whirl, Chromacolor, Decoy, Drift, Yellow Trumpet, Lemon Drops, Rosy Cloud. "What are they for?"

"We're going to plant them. They're daffodils. Well, they don't exactly look like daffodils right now. They're only bulbs."

Plant? I peer inside the bag marked "Drift." There must be more than thirty bulbs in it. I limp over to the next bag, "Lemon Drops," and there's more in this one than the first.

"Don't look so startled, Margaret," Mrs. Reynolds says. "It doesn't suit your face."

I grab a few bulbs from the next bag, the one marked "Audubon." Behind me Mrs. Reynolds says, "Don't even bother picking them up right away. You need a plan first."

"A plan?"

"Of course. Have you ever planted before?"

"Just some herbs in preschool. But that was in a little planter we took home for Mother's Day."

"No bulbs?"

I shake my head.

Mrs. Reynolds looks worried. "Let me tell you something about daffodils, Margaret. They're fragrant, beautiful, and hardy."

I scan the eight bags lined up. "These are *all* daffodils?"

"Oh, yes. But they each have their own unique scent and personality."

Wow. I don't know much about flowers in general, let alone details. My favorites were dandelions, because when we were younger, Leah and I used to search and pull all the dandelions from our neighbors' lawns, sing *Mama had a baby and her head popped off,* and flick the tops of the flowers off of the stems as we sang the word *popped*. Although, to be technical, dandelions aren't flowers. They're weeds.

"You'll need a shovel to start with," my employer says, interrupting my daydream. "I think there's one in the garage."

I place the bulbs back in their respective bags, then head for the detached garage in the back of the yard. It's a large, two-story structure. Yellow paint, though cracking and peeling from years of neglect, indicates this had once been a place of pride. There are stairs on the side, leading to the second level. Dirty, dusty windows outline the upstairs room. Is it an office of some sort? A private room?

The garage door is closed, so I have to lift it using my own strength, which isn't easy. With a loud creak of protest, the door finally lifts to reveal a large, black Cadillac parked inside. The place is dark and full of spider webs. Which means the place is full of spiders.

I'm not fond of either.

Maggie, you can do this. As I venture farther into the darkness, my eyes do the spider-scan. My mom used to make fun of me that I had peripheral vision specially designed to detect eight-legged creatures.

A shovel hangs on the wall, not far from the entrance. Good. I slowly inch forward, reaching out to grab the handle. Once I hold it, I let out a breath I didn't even know I'd been holding. I scurry out of the garage and head back to Mrs. Reynolds, sure at least a few webs have managed to stick to me.

"I got it," I say, holding out the shovel like a prized trophy.

The woman doesn't look impressed. "First, we'll have to prepare the soil."

I walk over to the empty flower beds and start poking the shovel into the dirt to loosen it. I do this for a few minutes. It's not so bad.

Mrs. Reynolds sneaks up behind me. "Wait."

I turn around. The woman is holding out a long, pink and green flower-print robe.

"What is *that*?" I ask.

"My muumuu. Put it on. It'll keep your clothes clean."

"Mrs. Reynolds, I can't wear that."

"Why not?"

Mrs. Reynolds clutches the muumuu, a big, ugly

housedress. I'm self-conscious enough as it is without wearing something my great-aunt Henrietta probably has in her closet.

"It's . . . it's not my size," I say lamely.

"Don't be a ninny, muumuus fit everyone. One size fits all. Put it on."

Reluctantly, I take the muumuu and slide the material over my head. The dress hangs on me like a tent.

Mrs. Reynolds steps back and surveys me. "Perfect."

I smile weakly at her.

"Okay, let's get to work."

For the next forty minutes Mrs. Reynolds directs me on how big to dig the holes, how to measure the extra soil needed in the bottom of the holes to create a pillow for the bulbs, and the best way to plant the bulbs—not in rows but scattered five inches apart.

I'm sweating now, and I fear Mrs. Reynolds is just getting started. But I'll do anything to keep this job. If it means creating pillows for her precious bulbs for the next few weeks until colder weather bears down on us, that's just fine. I can handle anything if the end result is earning the money to get away.

Sitting back, I wipe the dirt from my face with the sleeve of the muumuu. "What's over there?" I ask, pointing to a pile of lumber.

"The gazebo that never happened."

"I was in a gazebo at the Botanic Gardens last year," I say, imagining a huge gazebo in the middle of the yard.

"It reminded me of that scene in *The Sound of Music* where Liesl's boyfriend sings 'Sixteen Going on Seventeen' to her."

Mrs. Reynolds looks longingly at the pile. "Yes, well, I'm afraid the wood will probably be sitting there long after I'm dead and buried."

"You should totally get someone to build it," I tell her excitedly. "I can imagine it, with a pointed roof and all."

"Let's take a break," she says. "No more talk about gazebos that will never be."

Oh, yeah, I forgot. No senseless chatter for Mrs. Reynolds.

Since the accident, trying to stand hasn't been easy. Being covered in a muumuu makes it that much harder. Especially when I have to extend my leg in front of me to get up.

"What're you doing?"

"Getting up."

Mrs. Reynolds waves her hands around as if her limbs can talk. "Usually people bend their legs when they do that."

"I can't bend my leg."

"Who says?"

I turn and look straight at Mrs. Reynolds. Is she kidding? Obviously I'm crippled. Okay, so not crippled. But I got hit by a car. I'll never be the same again.

"You bend your leg when you walk. Don't know why you can't bend it when you stand, that's all," she says.

I finally stand, then take a deep breath. I'm itching to say something, but can't. Mrs. Reynolds is the first person in over a year that treats me as though nothing is wrong with me. It's refreshing and frustrating at the same time.

SEVENTEEN

Caleb

Mom knocks on my door on Saturday night before she leaves for the annual Fall Festival.

"Are you sure you don't want to go, Caleb? It'll be fun."

Yeah, right. "I'm sure."

"Leah's coming, too."

How the hell did Mom manage that? Leah lives in her room as if she's a bear in perpetual hibernation. I think I've seen her more in the halls at school than I have at home. "I'm gonna stay home and hang out," I say. There's no way I want to go to the fair and be one of the main attractions.

Mom opens the door and peeks her head inside. "Your father and I would like you to make an appearance. Dr. and Mrs. Tremont are going to be there. Your dad relies on his referrals. Put on one of the new outfits I bought and show off the clean-cut person you are."

I don't feel like dressing up in clothes that make me choke, and putting on another fake "happy" show. "Is that what you really want?"

She nods. "I do."

"Fine, I'll meet you there later," I say curtly. This bullshit is wearing me down fast.

"Thanks, Caleb. I appreciate it," she says, as if she's talking to a colleague.

Who is this lady who I used to call Mom? I need to make her realize I'm the same person as before. She can love the old Caleb Becker without trying to create a new and improved one.

After my parents and Leah leave, I head outside and make myself some chicken on the grill. I'm gonna eat here in my comfortable, ripped jeans and t-shirt before I dress up like a banker and head to the fairgrounds.

I'm sitting at the patio table when I hear a familiar voice.

"I thought I might find you out here."

I turn to my ex-girlfriend. Kendra looks great, dressed in a tight, pink shirt and short, white skirt. No trace of conservativeness in her attire, that's for sure.

"You're not going to the fair?" I ask.

She comes up real close to me and bends down. "I went, but you weren't there," she says in a sexy whisper.

"Did you want me to be?"

"No, because I want you all to myself. You're a legend in Paradise. Everybody's clamoring for a glimpse of the mysterious and dangerous Caleb Becker."

"Is that what they think, that I'm dangerous?"

"I'm just reporting the rumor. You *were* in jail, you know. I heard a lot of things happened to you when you were there to make you change."

"And what do you think?" I ask, confused by her motives for coming here. "Do you think I'm dangerous?"

"Absolutely." She's looking straight at me, but I sense she's thinking about something else. "Was it really as tough as they say?"

"Sometimes."

She twirls her blond curls around her finger. "Did you think about me?"

"Just about every day," I admit. "What about you?"

She smiles. "I missed you. But I couldn't handle what happened."

"Don't sweat it, Kend. That night was totally fucked up."

"You're telling me."

I look at her sideways. I've been dying to know the answer to this question. "Do you remember what happened?"

She blinks twice before answering. "Not much. I was almost as plastered as you were and ran when the cops came. My dad *is* the mayor, you know. His daughter couldn't be caught in the middle of that whole messy scene."

"Uh huh."

"I didn't expect you'd go to jail, Caleb. I just . . . it freaked me out."

"Freaked me out, too. But I'm back now."

"You sure are."

My ego needs me to ask this next question. It's strange, but this discussion is our way of figuring out where each of us stand in this relationship. "Have you been with anyone else?"

"Not anyone that matters."

What the hell does that mean? I'm not jealous. Okay, I am. *But she's here with you now,* a voice inside my head tells me.

And I missed her so much. Too much. I've dreamt about kissing her again, those full lips on mine, rubbing against her until I think I'll die from the sheer pleasure of it.

"Come here," I say, moving my chair out so she can sit on my lap. My libido kicks into gear, ready for this immediately. "It's been a long time, Kend, but I'm game if you are."

She settles herself on my thighs and wraps her arms around my neck. I watch her lips with interest as she smiles at me. Wet, shiny lips from whatever she put on them before she came over.

Whoever made *that* glossy lip shit up is a genius.

I take the curled ends of her golden hair between my fingers and twist them between my thumb and forefinger. Her hair feels different than I remember. It used to be softer. I always loved playing with it. "You changed the color," I say.

"It's lighter. Do you like it?"

What can I say, that it feels more like straw than silk? "I need time to get used to it."

I know I should have kissed her by now, but I'm hesitating. I've kissed Kendra a thousand times before. She's an awesome kisser, and those lips are begging to be messed with. So what's my problem?

She feels the top of my buzz cut with her palm. "I hope you'll grow out your hair. I can't grab onto it now."

"We'll see."

"So noncommittal, aren't you." She laughs, then says, "I missed you, CB."

If she missed me so much, why do I have this strange feeling she's holding something back? Shit, I've got to stop playing mind games with myself and overanalyzing stuff. I know what'll make me stop thinking.

I put my hand on the back of Kendra's head and guide her mouth toward mine. As my lips touch hers, the scent of cherries from the glossy stuff is overpowering.

In a bad way.

My lips and tongue slide against hers, but all I can think about is that I hate cherries. I hate cherry pie, I hate cherries in my fruit cocktail or on top of a hot fudge sundae. I even hate Cherry Coke.

Kendra moans while our mouths are still meshed. Her tongue is working overtime and she twists her body so she's straddling me.

I open my eyes while we're kissing. My gaze focuses on Maggie Armstrong's room. Now not only do I have cherry lips attached to mine, I'm hoping Maggie Armstrong doesn't see me lip-locked and tongue-tied with Kendra.

Don't even ask me why I care.

I pull back and say, "Let's go inside."

Kendra slides off my lap, and we hold hands as I lead her to my bedroom. I wipe off my lips with the back of my hand, hoping the cherry flavor will disappear.

Kendra lies on my bed when we reach my room, not even hesitating or questioning why we're moving so fast after not being together for a year. "It's just like old times," she says.

Except somehow it doesn't feel as exciting or daring as it used to. Maybe it's because we're older now.

I take my shirt off, then slip into bed next to her. She starts kissing my chest. "Jeez, Caleb. Your pecs are huge."

With my forefinger I lightly wiggle her new, shiny bellybutton ring. "I guess we both changed, huh?"

"Let me investigate how much." She kisses her way down, past my chest and stops at the waistband of my jeans.

When she starts unbuttoning them, I put my hand over hers to stop her.

She looks up at me, confused. I don't blame her. I'm all screwed up in the head and need to take everything slower than before. I swear, a year ago I'd be jumping her bones before we even reached my room.

"What's wrong?" she says.

I shake my head, rub my hand over my hair, and take a deep breath. Fuck. I'm screwing everything up.

She rests her head on my shoulder and places her arm across my stomach. It feels real good and I'm glad she doesn't make me talk about it. Maybe she gets it, maybe she understands I can't verbalize my fucked-up thoughts. But then she starts getting restless after a few minutes and sits up. "I should probably go back to the festival before my parents find out where I've gone."

In the end she doesn't understand. Just like everyone else.

With a flip of her hair over her shoulders, she slips her shoes back on and stands up.

I convince myself things will get back to normal soon enough. I'm back home, I have my girl again. Okay, I'll admit things are strange between us. Her hair is fake, her lips taste different, and her kisses are frantic instead of sexy.

"I saw you talking to Samantha Hunter in the hall yesterday," she says, turning back and looking at me.

I sit up and lean against my headboard, still shirtless. "Yeah, she wanted to know if I'll wrestle this year."

Kendra blows out an annoyed breath. "You don't think she's cute, do you?"

I shrug. "She's all right, I guess."

"Because girls like that are totally manipulative."

"I'm not lookin' at other girls, Kend, if that's what you're worried about."

"That's good." The corners of her mouth turn up, but then she bites down on her lower lip. "I'm glad you're back, but . . ."

"But what?" I ask.

"Can we keep this thing between us a secret, Caleb? The kids at school are expecting a big show between you and me, and I don't want it to get weird. Besides, my dad is up for election in November and he's already forbidden me to have any contact with you. It'll be best if nobody knows about this right now."

Her comments shouldn't surprise me, but they do. I just say, "That's cool," because, well, what else can I say?

Following Kendra out to her car, I wonder what our lives would have been like if I hadn't been locked up. I wouldn't have to keep our relationship a damn secret, that's for sure.

When we're in the front yard, Kendra climbs into her car. Then she opens her purse and pulls out a tube of lip gloss. Twisting the rearview mirror, she carefully glides on more cherry gloss, essentially erasing away our power make-out session. When her lips are as glossy as when she came here, she drives off.

Shaking my head, I head back inside. I spot the picture of Kendra when I get to my room. Removing it from my headboard, I stare at it.

It's hard keeping everything the same when the same things look and feel so different.

EIGHTEEN

Maggie

I'm wearing a long print dress that touches the ground and a powder blue sweater over it. Mom bought me the dress because she knows how I feel about exposing any part of my left leg. Deep down I know she also hopes boys will see me as Maggie Armstrong and not as *the girl who got hit by Caleb Becker.* Guess what, it's not going to happen.

I didn't have the heart to tell her a pretty dress can't erase the ugly scars hiding underneath.

We head over to the Paradise County Fairgrounds. They've transformed the fairgrounds into an amusement park, complete with a Ferris wheel and dunking booth.

The Ladies' Auxiliary sponsors the festival each year. Usually the entire town attends.

The food pavilion is covered in twinkling lights, reminding me of Christmas.

Mom puts down the brownies she made on the potluck table, then scans the crowd. "Look, there's Lou," she says, pointing.

Sitting next to him is his mother, *my* boss. "Should we go say hi?" I ask.

Mom shrugs. "It would be nice."

When we reach the table, Mr. Reynolds stands up and smiles. "Linda, glad you made it. Hi, Maggie."

"Hi, Mr. Reynolds. Hi, Mrs. Reynolds."

Mr. Reynolds leans close and whispers in my ear, "We're not at the diner. You can call me Lou."

"That'd be weird," I say. Calling Mom's boss by his first name is just too . . . I don't know . . . familiar.

"Okay, well, when you don't feel weird about it give it a try."

Mom sits next to her boss and I walk around the table and plop down next to Mrs. Reynolds.

"Mrs. Reynolds, it was so generous of you to give my daughter a job," Mom says. "As I told you on the phone, I'm very grateful."

"I'm the grateful one," Mrs. Reynolds says. "We've had a productive first week. Haven't we, Margaret?"

My fingernails still have dirt under them that I haven't

been able to scrape out. "Mrs. Reynolds is an expert on daffodils, Mom."

"When you get back from Spain they'll be up and blooming," Mrs. Reynolds says.

I smile, thinking about leaving for Spain. It's about the only thing making me smile lately.

Mrs. Reynolds looks longingly at the buffet table. "I'm famished," she says. "How about we take a gander at the food and see if there's anything worthwhile."

"Mom, don't stuff yourself," Mr. Reynolds says over the loud dance music the band just started to play on the makeshift stage in front of the Fun House.

Mrs. Reynolds rolls her eyes. "My son thinks I'm a child."

"Mom, you know what the—" Mr. Reynolds' gruff voice chimes in.

Mrs. Reynolds silences her son with a single stare. Mom looks kind of nervous and I feel the same way. I don't want to get involved in this. It's clearly out of my jurisdiction as companion.

Mr. Reynolds turns to my mom. "Linda, how about showing the teens some old dance moves?"

Wow, that came out of left field. Mom never dances. She and my dad would come to the festival year after year and I never once saw them sway to the music, let alone dance.

"I'd love to," Mom says. "Maggie, you don't mind, do you?"

When I shake my head, she takes Mr. Reynolds' outstretched hand and he leads her away from the food pavilion.

I'm sitting here with my eyes wide open. What just happened? Did my mom accept a dance with her boss?

Isn't that illegal?

I can see the dance floor from where I'm sitting. Right away, Mom is wiggling her body and moving around like a teenager. I scan the fairgrounds to see if anyone else is paying attention. Sure enough, a group of kids from school are watching her.

I want to die.

Why would Mom want to dance in the first place? She's making a spectacle of herself, jumping around as if she doesn't care people are staring. Isn't it bad enough people stare at me?

"Margaret, I'm ready to load up my plate now that my son who thinks he's a doctor is out of my hair. Will you help me?"

I tear my gaze away from the dancing queen. "Uh, yeah, sure."

Mrs. Reynolds leans on her cane as we head to the food line. I hold her plate and pile food on as she points to various dishes. The old lady is totally oblivious to the scene on the dance floor.

"What do you keep staring at?" Mrs. Reynolds asks.

"Nothing."

"That nothing's getting a lot of attention."

I make a harrumph and move down the line. But when I get to Mrs. Becker's famous Spaghetti Spectacular, I freeze and wonder if Leah and Caleb are here.

"This one looks good," Mrs. Reynolds says, referring to the spaghetti dish.

"It tastes good, too," I admit. "But can you eat it? Mr. Reynolds said—"

"Margaret, I'm an old lady who enjoys her food. If I can't eat what I want, you might as well bury me six feet under right here and now."

"Okaay," I say warily. "If you insist." I place a small spoonful on Mrs. Reynolds' plate, but she raises her eyebrows and urges me to heap on another spoonful. When we get to the end of the buffet line, I'm afraid to take another glance at the dance floor.

It's like a car wreck. You know what you're going to see is bad, but you can't help it. I wonder if that's how people felt when they saw me lying on the ground after the accident.

Okay, so I'm just like everyone else. I check out the dance floor and, thankfully, my mom is nowhere to be found. But I do see Kendra Greene. She's slow dancing with Brian Newcomb as if he were the love of her life.

My dream is to find a guy who'll love me despite my flaws and won't turn away from me when a perfect girl walks by. Maybe a boy like that doesn't even exist.

I'm sitting at the table watching Mrs. Reynolds eat. I have no clue how she packs it all in for such a small woman. She takes a small bite of the Spaghetti Spectacular and gives me a nod. "It's like a burst of flavor and different textures making it taste . . ."

"Spectacular?" I say.

"Quite," she agrees, and we both laugh.

Mom comes sidling over to the table. Was that a shimmy I just saw her do as she sat down?

"What's so funny?" Mom asks.

"The spaghetti dish," Mrs. Reynolds says. "It *is* spectacular."

There's silence now, because Mom immediately knows we're talking about Mrs. Becker's award-winning specialty.

Mr. Reynolds is sweating and takes a sip of water. "Is something wrong?"

Mom shakes her head.

The band guy is yelling for the over-twenty-one crowd to get on the dance floor. Parents flock to the middle of the floor, ready to show off their moves.

I watch the other kids in my grade running around and enjoying themselves. Brian and Kendra enter the Fun House. Drew Rudolph is trying to coax Brianne onto the Tilt-A-Whirl. My cousin Sabrina is sitting next to her sister on the Ferris wheel.

"Go on," Mrs. Reynolds says. "Join your friends."

"I don't have friends," I admit. "I'm what you call a loser. Or a loner. Take your pick."

"Pshaw."

"Huh?"

"Pshaw. Hogwash. You're a smart, pretty young lady. Girls like you are not losers. Or loners."

"I'm not pretty, that's for sure. And I limp."

She looks me up and down. "You may lack fashion

sense, but you have fine features when you're not pouting or looking startled. And the limp . . . as long as it doesn't bother you, it shouldn't matter what people think."

I believe I have that startled look on my face right now.

"And what's this nonsense about you not having any friends? Everyone should have at least one friend."

I glance around and spot Leah Becker, sitting alone at one of the tables. Her parents are in a deep conversation with another couple a few feet away. I would walk up to her, but she'd probably ignore me.

Mrs. Reynolds puts her hand on mine. "Is she a friend?"

"Used to be."

"Go talk to her."

"I wouldn't even know what to say."

Mrs. Reynolds lets out a frustrated breath. "Suit yourself, child. But when you're an old bird like me you'll be wishing you had more friends in your life. Being alone isn't fun, is it?"

"No. Being alone isn't fun."

I look over at my mom, who is now line dancing. She doesn't look alone. In fact, she hasn't looked this happy for a long time. Mom smiles at Mr. Reynolds and he smiles back.

Mr. Reynolds. Lou. My mom's boss. My boss' son. Well, whatever his name is, it's clear to me he has the hots for my mom.

I don't know if I should be embarrassed, angry, or happy for her.

NINETEEN

Caleb

M y pants are too fucking tight and this shirt has so much starch in it I feel like a mannequin. But I'm here, at the Fall Festival. Once I'm done acting like the model son, I'm outta here.

I spot my parents by the food pavilion, talking with another couple. Nothing has changed since I've been back. My sister is still a zombie, but it's worse now, because since she ran out of the lunchroom Monday, she's ignored me. My parents haven't brought up the accident since I've been back. I tried to talk about it, but I've been shut down.

When I walk up to my parents, my mom smiles. "We were waiting for you, Caleb."

"Well, I'm here," I say unenthusiastically, not in the least ready to put on this show.

My dad looks tired; there are circles under his eyes and he's not walking as tall and straight as I remember. "Caleb, do you remember Dr. and Mrs. Tremont? Dr. Tremont owns a dental practice in Denton, and just opened one up in Paradise now that Dr. Kryzanowich retired."

"Really?"

Dr. Tremont points to the east. "Over by Central and Carriagedale Roads. You know, the new building next to the Paradise cinemas."

I shake my head. "I haven't seen it yet."

"Where have you been hiding out?" Dr. Tremont says, laughing. "It's the building with the big tooth out front."

My dad is turning red under his collar. "I'm starving," he says before I tell Dr. Tremont that I haven't seen his big toothed building because I've been locked up in jail for the past year. "Why don't you taste some of my wife's dish while Caleb *finds his friends.*"

Mom does a really good job of directing the Tremonts to the buffet table and away from me. Do you think Mom realizes it wasn't the best idea to try and pretend like I'm a perfect son? My sister joins them, totally ignoring me.

The Fall Festival is a zoo. It's hard to believe Paradise is a small town when there are so many people around. Brian and the guys are hanging out near the parking lot.

"Wow, Caleb, who dressed you?" Brian quips, shaking his head in disbelief.

I grimace. "Would you believe it if I told you my mother did?"

Brian nods. "Yeah. Paradise wasn't the same without you, man. But those clothes have *got* to go."

Drew chuckles while he lights a cigarette. "You're right, Brian. Paradise isn't the same. I saw Mrs. Armstrong dancing with that guy from the diner. They looked pretty tight. Do you think they're . . . you, know? God knows Maggie's not gettin' any. That girl needs a bunch more surgeries before she'll attract any dude. Maybe she could get a prom date over the internet."

Nobody laughs, because Drew is not funny. He's been a jerk ever since I came back, trying his best to piss me off on purpose.

Tristan throws a football in the air. "We're heading over to the field to play ball. Let's go before our moms try to make us dance with them."

I take off the ridiculous shirt while I play, but my balls are being strangled by the pants I'm wearing. After forty-five minutes, we head back. But when Tristan and Brian are ahead of us, I grab Drew by the shoulder and push him back into a tree. I take him completely off guard. He has no clue I'm tempted to kick his ass. One thing I learned at the DOC from the inmates . . . take them when they least expect it.

"Here's the deal," I say low and harsh as I grab his shirt and twist it up close to his throat. "You stop bringing up Maggie or jail or the accident. Got it? If you want to keep running your mouth off, that's fine, but next time you do it you'll find my fist in it. Guaranteed."

"I was just kidding," Drew chokes out, a faint thread of hysteria in his voice. "Jeez, Caleb, lighten up."

I let go of his shirt, but give him one last warning. "Up until two weeks ago I was living with a bunch of gang members. Don't tell me to lighten up."

———

It's Thursday night, five days after the festival. I'm in Kendra's bedroom while her parents are at some dinner function. We're supposed to study; we've both got tests tomorrow.

Unfortunately, I realized about a half hour ago she's not interested in studying. Kendra is strutting in front of me, modeling different outfits she bought at the mall yesterday. "Well . . ." she says, showing off a designer dress. "What do you think?"

I'm busy reading about the *Magna Carta*. "I can't flunk this test, Kend."

She puts her hands on her hips and pouts. "I swear you pay more attention to the girls at school than you do to me."

I look up from my book. "Are you kidding me?"

"No. Samantha Hunter is, like, lusting after you during gym class and you're falling for it. And I heard you and Emily Steinway were having a pretty intense conversation in biology."

"I haven't said two words to Samantha, Kend. And Emily and I are bio partners. What are you doing, spying on me? I'd be glad to tell everyone we're back together. You're the one who wants to keep our relationship a damn secret."

This week we've met at the forest preserve, under the high school bleachers, and now I had to enter her house through the back door so none of her neighbors would see me coming in. I'm sick of sneaking around.

"I told you my father is up for election in November, Caleb. His daughter can't be seen dating an ex-con."

She says it so easily. There's not a speck of apology or hesitation in her voice as she spurts out the word "ex-con." "I gotta go," I say, then close my history book.

She comes toward me, placing her hand on my chest. "Don't go. I'll make it worth your while."

"What are you talking about?"

She slowly pulls the spaghetti straps off her shoulder, revealing bare skin. A few seconds later she's stripped her dress off and is standing in front of me wearing only a black lace bra and matching thong.

My gaze travels over her creamy white skin. Hell, yeah, I want this. But she's not acting like a girlfriend. She doesn't have to strip to keep me here. She doesn't have to use her body to lure me. This is so fucked up. "Kendra . . ."

She steps toward me, putting her finger on my lips to stop me from talking. "Shh, I hear my parents in the hallway," she whispers.

Shit.

Sure enough there's a knock on her bedroom door a

second later. "Kendra, you home?" her mom says through the door.

"Uh, yeah," Kendra says loudly as she picks up her discarded dress. "Caleb, get in the closet," she whispers.

This is seriously not happening. "I'm not getting in the closet," I say. There's no way I'm going to get locked up again, even in my girlfriend's closet instead of a cell.

"Shh, they're going to hear you."

Her mom knocks again and says, "Who are you talking to? Kendra, open the door."

Kendra scurries to get her dress back on. "Nobody, Mom, I just have the radio on. I'm getting dressed. I'll be out in a minute, okay?"

"Hurry up. Senator Boyle came all the way back here to meet you," her mom says, then I hear footsteps moving away from the door.

"When are you going to tell them we're together?" I ask Kendra. "After the election?"

"Can we talk about that later?" she whispers as she quickly checks out her appearance in her mirror. I watch as she rolls massive amounts of lip gloss on her lips. Cherry flavor wafts to my nostrils and I wonder how long I can be stuck in this cherry-scented room before I pass out.

I open the window.

"Caleb, what are you doing?"

I throw my history book to the ground below, praying it'll still be intact when I retrieve it. Then I heave one foot over the ledge. "Leaving."

"It's a two-story house. You'll kill yourself."

I'm not about to hide in her room like a prisoner. Besides, if I jump hard enough and high enough, I just might be able to catch a branch on the tree a few feet away from the window.

She runs toward me. "Don't, CB."

I stare right into her blue eyes. *Why, not? Because you love me, because you don't want me to get hurt . . . because you want to take me downstairs and announce to your parents and their friends that no matter what happened in the past, we're together and nobody can separate us?*

"I'll get into trouble if they see you," she announces.

"See you on the other side," I say to Kendra before standing on the window ledge, saying a quick prayer, and taking a leap.

TWENTY

Maggie

Mrs. Reynolds is waiting for me on the back swing with the muumuu in hand when I get to her house, just like she's done since my first day on the job. I tried protesting the offending garment with no success. So now I put it on and look like a complete dork as I'm working.

It's not like I need to worry about looking good, anyway. Caleb and his friends said the only way I'd even get a date for prom was to advertise on the internet. I heard them at the Fall Festival talking about me. I cried that night because I can't turn back the clock and erase what happened. Caleb stood there with the guys as if he had nothing to do with making me this way. His non-reaction hurt more than Drew's words.

"Today we're going to clean the attic," Mrs. Reynolds announces. "Here, take this broom. I'll bring the dustpan and pail."

"What about planting bulbs?" I ask.

"I'm sick of looking at bulbs. We can continue planting tomorrow."

She leads me up the stairway to the attic. "Don't close the door, it'll lock us in."

"That's dangerous," I say. And scary, like something out of a horror movie. There's a door stopper that she puts in place before we enter. It's a small, dark place filled with boxes and pictures and . . . spider webs. "Mrs. Reynolds?"

"Yes, Margaret."

"I'm afraid of spiders."

"Why?"

"Because they have eight creepy legs, they bite, and they have sticky string that comes out of their butts to capture bugs before they suck their blood."

I think Mrs. Reynolds is going to laugh at me. But she doesn't. Instead she says, "Spiders control the insect population. They're a necessity and that's all there is to it."

While that might be true, I still don't like them. But that doesn't stop Mrs. Reynolds from leading me farther into the attic—pail, dustpan and all. I'm ready to go into a rendition of "It's a Hard Knock Life." I look around. This attic is definitely creepy—large trunks in one corner and moving boxes in the other.

Mrs. Reynolds finds an old chair and sits in it. "You can start by dusting the trunks first."

Thank God those are in the middle of the floor, untouched by webs. The old lady is totally prepared. She pulls a rag and a can of Endust out of the pail. I spray the top of a wooden trunk, cleaning it until it shines.

"Open it," Mrs. Reynolds says.

I look at her, unsure.

"Go on."

I unhook the latch, lift the top, and peer inside.

The first thing I see is a framed picture of a man and woman. "Is this you?"

"Yes, with my late husband, Albert, may he rest in peace."

In the picture a much younger Mrs. Reynolds is wearing a knee-length tailored dress and satin gloves that go up over her elbows. Mr. Reynolds isn't even looking into the camera, he's gazing at Mrs. Reynolds as if she were a rare diamond. "Did you get married young?"

"I was twenty and he was twenty-four. We were very much in love."

I hand the picture to her. "I wish my parents loved each other. They're divorced."

"Yes, well, life does keep going on, doesn't it?"

"Yep." Even after the accident, when I knew I'd never

be able to walk normally again or play tennis anymore, life kept rolling on.

Whether I wanted it to or not.

Mrs. Reynolds leans over and studies more pictures. "I've spent a little time with your mother at Auntie Mae's," she says while studying a picture of a little boy. "She's a lovely lady."

"Thanks," I say, proud of Mom. She's cool, for a mom. I just wish my dad thought she was *lovely* enough to want to stay married to her.

Mrs. Reynolds hands me the picture of the little boy. "That's my son."

I almost laugh at the picture. Who thought this little boy would grow up and one day be my mom's boss?

"He was married once. She died of ovarian cancer five years later." She sighs.

"They didn't have any kids?" I ask.

She shakes her head. "Okay, enough dawdling. I have a bunch of boxes that need to be tossed. Why don't we pile them in a corner so they can easily be spotted and taken to the trash. Somewhere around here are boxes labeled 'taxes'." She points to one of the corners of the attic. "I think they're over there."

I walk over to the boxes and do the spider-scan. Eek. Webs line the ceiling corners, just waiting for an unsuspecting insect to fly by. I don't even see the spiders. It's like they're undercover spies until their prey struggles, hopelessly stuck in the web.

I shudder just thinking about it. Thank God I'm not an insect.

"Margaret?"

"Yes."

"I'm getting older every second, you know."

I put my hands in the sleeves of the muumuu and shove boxes aside with muumuu-covered fists. I'm trying not to think about my leg and how I'm going to maneuver around the boxes with spiders staring down at me from the ceiling.

I've made a path and head behind the stack of boxes. I check out an orange, plastic container made to look like a picnic basket. "What kind of boxes are they? Bankers boxes or moving boxes?" I ask.

"I don't remember, but I'm pretty certain they're labeled."

Okay. I start turning boxes around, hoping to find the words TAXES on the front.

I shriek when I hear something behind me.

Spinning around, I see it's only Mrs. Reynolds.

"Oh, calm yourself," she chides. "Did you find any?"

"I think so." I pick up a box marked *TAXES, 1968*. "Is this one?"

She claps her hands, like a teacher would do if a student gets an answer correct. "Yes. Put it by the door. There's so many to toss, I think this may take a few days."

As soon as I place the first box in the "toss" pile, the

doorbell rings. Mrs. Reynolds doesn't hear it. "Someone's ringing the doorbell," I say.

She furrows her brows and tilts her head to listen for it. "I don't hear it, but then again these ears are about as good as my eyes. Be a doll and answer it, would you?"

"Sure." I head down the stairs. The doorbell rings two more times before I can get to the door. I open it quickly, then stumble backwards. Because the last person I expected to see standing in front of me is Caleb Becker.

And, for the second time since he's been back, he reaches out to touch me.

TWENTY-ONE

Caleb

I swear, *my* leg almost just gave out on me. Because the last person I expected to answer the door to Mrs. Reynolds' house was Maggie Armstrong wearing a ridiculous, oversized dress with pink and green flowers plastered all over it.

I try and grab her arm when she loses her balance, but I'm too late. Once on the floor, she refuses my outstretched hand.

"Wh . . . What are you doing here?"

"What are *you* doing here?" I ask.

"I work here after school," she says while trying to pretend she's content to stay sprawled on the floor.

I quickly shove my Justice Department ID in my back

pocket. I double-check the address again before saying, "I'm here to see a Mrs. Reynolds. This *is* her house, isn't it?" Maggie's hatred is evident in her stare. "Listen, seeing you here is a surprise to me, too," I say. "The manager at The Trusty Nail sent me. This lady's house is the next job site on the list."

I watch as Maggie pulls herself up. It's painful, I can tell just by watching her fingers curl into a tight fist.

God, watching her struggle is making me sick to my stomach. Because I indirectly did this to her. "I'm sorry," I say.

"Tell it to the judge," she mumbles.

"I did," I respond truthfully. Not that it mattered to Judge Farkus. The guy wanted to make me an example for all delinquents who drank then got behind the wheel of a car. "What do you want from me, Maggie?"

"I want you to leave."

"I can't," I tell her.

An old lady appears from the back of the house and shuffles to the door. "You must be from the community service program," she says.

"Yes, ma'am." I introduce myself and hand her my community service ID for inspection. It's a requirement to show it before entering a house.

Mrs. Reynolds scans my ID, then hands it back. "Well, come on in. This here's Margaret, my companion. Margaret this is . . . what did you say your name was again?"

"Caleb."

Mrs. Reynolds tells Maggie, "Caleb is going to help us. Show him to the attic and explain our project while I check on some cookies I have baking in the oven."

I set my backpack on the ground after Mrs. Reynolds is out of sight. "Another awkward situation, huh?"

Maggie is as still as a statue.

"I wish you never came back," she says quietly, hugging herself.

I'm tempted to leave and face Damon's wrath for ditching community service, but I won't. I'm stuck here with her.

"I'm not going anywhere until I finish this job for the lady."

Maggie's eyes widen. Her mouth opens and closes, but no words come out. She turns around and walks farther into the house.

I silently follow her up a narrow staircase on the second floor to the attic.

Maggie points to a box. "That needs to be thrown out. I'll put boxes there and you can dispose of them."

I nod.

We work in silence. Maggie places the boxes in the discard pile and I carry them down the stairs. Mrs. Reynolds has me stuff the boxes in huge garbage bags and then lug them to the recycle bin at the end of the driveway.

Mrs. Reynolds comes out of the kitchen and hands me a plate of cookies. "Here, bring these up to the attic. You and Maggie can share them while you work."

I enter the attic for what seems like the hundredth time today with the cookies in hand. Maggie throws a box in my direction, but I move out of the way to avoid it. It was intentional, no doubt about it. "Watch it, will ya?" I drop the plate on a trunk in the middle of the attic.

She turns her back to me and ignores the plate.

Maggie thinks she's the only victim in this whole mess. But I have to keep my cool. No matter what happens, I can't let her get under my skin and let the truth come out.

"Listen, Maggie, it was an accident. If I could take back that day, I would. If I could turn back time, I would."

She turns to me now, her head tilted to the side. "Tell me, Caleb. Why does your apology sound so hollow to me?"

I stand, speechless, as she takes the plate of cookies and leaves the attic. Why can't this be easy? I pick up the next box and don't look up until all the boxes are trashed.

Maggie leaves Mrs. Reynolds' house first, but I stay behind. The old lady is in the backyard when I hand her the completion sheet and pen. "Thanks for letting me work here," I say.

"My husband, Albert, may he rest in peace, felt it important to help out the less fortunate. Don't get me started on the juvenile justice system or we'll be here for weeks. You did a good job today."

I flash her a smile of appreciation.

She starts to sign the form, but stops herself. "It says here you have experience in construction. You know . . . I may have another job for you. That is, if you're up to it."

"What kind of job?"

"How good are you with your hands?"

"Better than most," I say, then chuckle.

The old lady points to a tall pile of lumber stacked in the corner of the backyard. "Okay, Mr. Better-Than-Most. You think you could build me a gazebo out of this pile of old wood? You *do* know what a gazebo is, don't you?"

Yeah, I know what one is. Building a gazebo will take at least a couple of weeks, probably even fill up enough time to finish my community service.

What am I thinking? I can't work with Maggie. No way. It would never work.

Although it's not like I'd actually be working *with* her. I'll be on my own, building the gazebo. The way Mrs. Reynolds is looking at me with confidence strengthens my bruised ego. I'm not thinking about Maggie. I'm not thinking about what's right or wrong. I blurt out, "I can do it." I should be honest with the lady and tell her about why I was convicted. And, more importantly, who I was convicted of hitting. "Mrs. Reynolds, I have to be honest with you . . ."

As if on cue, the phone rings. The old lady takes her cane and hurries into the house. "Just come back tomorrow and we'll finish our conversation then."

So now I run to catch the bus because I'm late. When I get on, Maggie is sitting up front so I head for the rear.

The fifteen-minute bus ride seems like an hour. At our

stop, we're the only two left on the bus. We get off and I let her lead the way while I follow behind.

My sister is outside. The expression on her face when she sees Maggie and me walking up the street together is priceless.

"Did you just come home with Maggie?" Leah asks, following me into the house.

"We were on the same bus. Don't get all hyped up about it."

"Don't get all hyped up about what?" my mom says, coming into the room in the middle of a conversation I don't want her to know anything about.

"It's nothing," I tell Mom, then narrow my eyes at my sister and say through clenched teeth so only she can hear, "so stop making a big deal about it."

Leah runs up to her room and slams her door shut. My mom goes back into the kitchen, totally oblivious.

The Beckers are a picture-perfect family. A picture-perfect, royally-fucked-up family.

TWENTY-TWO

Maggie

On Monday I head for the bus after school. As I step into the aisle, I catch sight of Caleb already sitting in the back. It was bad enough working side by side in that small attic last week. If I have to work with him again I'll quit.

But then I won't be going to Spain.

And if I don't go to Spain, I won't be leaving Paradise next semester.

And if I don't leave Paradise next semester, Caleb and his friends will be laughing all the way to prom while I sit home and prove them right.

Maybe he's not going to Mrs. Reynolds' house today and I'm going off on unnecessary tangents for no reason.

Maybe he's working somewhere else doing odd jobs. But as he follows me into Mrs. Reynolds' backyard, my fears are realized.

"Now come inside, both of you. Irina brought over some pie." Mrs. Reynolds walks into the house, not realizing that neither me nor Caleb has followed her.

"Took you long enough," Mrs. Reynolds says when I enter the kitchen. "Here, I cut some pie for both of you."

I sit down at the kitchen table and stare at the pie. Normally I'd dig right in, but I can't. Caleb walks in and sits across from me. I focus my attention in the opposite direction, as if the painting of the fruit bowl on the wall is the most interesting object I've ever laid eyes on.

"Margaret, remember you told me I should have that gazebo built?"

"Yeah," I answer cautiously.

Mrs. Reynolds holds her chin up. "Well, Caleb is going to help make that a reality. It may take a few weeks, but—"

A few weeks? "If he stays, I quit," I blurt out. A few *weeks?*

I hear the clink of Caleb's fork hitting the plate, then he stands and storms out of the room.

Mrs. Reynolds puts her hands on either side of her face and says, "Margaret, what is all this nonsense about you quitting? Why?"

"I can't work with him, Mrs. Reynolds. He did this to me," I cry.

"Did what, child?"

"I went to jail for hitting Maggie with my car while I was drunk," Caleb says, reappearing in the doorway.

Mrs. Reynolds makes some tsking noises, then says, "My, my, we are in a pickle, aren't we?"

I look up at Mrs. Reynolds with pleading eyes. "Just make him leave."

I can tell she's going to do it, she's going to tell Caleb to get out.

Mrs. Reynolds walks up to Caleb and says, "You have to understand that my first priority is Margaret. I'll call the senior center and have them contact your community service officer."

"Please, Mrs. Reynolds," Caleb tells her, his voice pleading. "I just want to finish the job and just . . . be free again."

Mrs. Reynolds looks back at me, her wise eyes telling me more than words could say. *Forgive.*

I can't forgive. I've tried. If he'd innocently lost control of the car and hit me, it would have been forgivable. I don't know how innocent the accident was. God, I can't believe in my heart of hearts he deliberately hit me with the car. But too many questions have gone unanswered.

Questions I want to remain unanswered.

They said he left me lying in the street as if I were an animal. *That* is unforgivable. I don't know if I can ever get over it.

Because it reminds me too much of what my father

did. He left me without looking back. And worse, Caleb destroyed the one chance I had to impress my dad. I push my way past Caleb and head to the attic, a place that's dark, secluded, and private. I'm not even thinking about black widow spiders as I open the attic door and hobble inside.

Gosh, I used to worship the ground Caleb walked on. He was tall, handsome . . . clearly one of the populars, where Leah's and my status teetered on the edge. As if that wasn't enough, nothing ever bothered the guy. Maybe it's because guys like him always get what they want, they never have to work hard for anything. Maybe, deep down, I'm glad he's having a hard time. And deep down I know it's selfish for me to think this way. I shouldn't thrive on someone else's unhappiness.

But as the saying goes, misery likes company. And I feel miserable, inside and out. Isn't it fair that the person who's miserable with me is the guy who made me this way?

Mrs. Reynolds followed me, I can tell by the powdery scent that travels with her.

"This is a mighty interesting place to hide out. I thought you were afraid of spiders."

"I am, but in the dark I can't see them. Is he gone?" I ask hopefully.

She shakes her head. "We need to talk."

"Do I have to?"

"Let's just put it this way. You're not leaving the attic until you hear me out."

Defeated, I sit on one of the trunks. "I'm listening."

"Good." She takes a seat on the chair, still left here from the other day. "I had one sibling," she says. "A sister named Lottie. She was younger than me, smarter than me, prettier than me, with long, slender legs and thick, black hair."

Mrs. Reynolds looks up at me and continues. "You see, I was the fat kid with bright red hair, the kid you look at and have to stop yourself from cringing. During summer break from college one year, I brought a boy to my parents' summer home. I'd lost weight, I wasn't in my sister's shadow anymore, and I finally started feeling like I was worth more than I ever thought I deserved."

I can picture it in my mind. "So you overcame your fears and fell in love?"

"I fell in love, all right, head over heels. His name was Fred." Mrs. Reynolds pauses, then sighs. "He treated me as though I was the most amazing girl he'd ever seen. Well, he did until my sister came to the summer house for a surprise visit." She looks directly at me and shrugs. "I found him kissing her by the docks the morning after she arrived."

"Oh my God."

"I hated her, blamed her for stealing my boyfriend. So I packed up, left, and never talked to either one of them again."

"You never talked to your sister again?" I ask. "Ever?"

"I didn't even attend their wedding two years later."

My mouth drops open. "She married Fred?"

"You got it. Had four kids, too."

"Where are they now?"

"I got a call from one of their kids that Lottie died a few years ago. Fred's in a nursing home with Alzheimer's. You know what the worst part is?"

I'm riveted by her story. "What?"

Mrs. Reynolds stands, then pats me on my knee. "That, my dear, is what you're going to have to figure out all by yourself."

"You think Caleb should stay and build the gazebo, don't you?" I ask when she starts walking to the door.

"I'll leave that decision up to you. He won't go back to jail if it doesn't work out, I would never let that happen. I just figure he's a boy who wants to right his wrongs, Margaret. He's waiting downstairs for your answer."

She walks out of the attic. I hear her orthopedic shoes shuffling as she takes each stair. Can I just stay here forever, living with the spiders and cobwebs and antique trunks filled with an old lady's memories?

I know the answer, even as I stand and head down the stairs to face the one person I've been dying to avoid.

He's sitting on the couch in the living room, leaning forward with his elbows resting on his knees. When he hears me enter the room, he looks up. "Well?"

I can tell he's not happy I have the control. Caleb used to always have the cards and knew which ones to play to get his way. Not this time. I'd love to tell him to leave. That's his punishment for not loving me back. But I know that would be idiotic, childish, and stupid. Besides, I don't love Caleb anymore. I don't even like him. I'm convinced he can't hurt me anymore, physically or emotionally. "You can stay."

He nods and starts to stand.

"Wait. I have two conditions."

His eyebrows raise up.

"One, you don't tell anyone about us working together. Two, you don't talk to me . . . I ignore you and you ignore me."

I think he's going to argue because his lip curls up and his eyebrows furrow as if he thinks I'm an idiot.

But then he says, "Fine. Done deal," and heads to the backyard.

I find Mrs. Reynolds in the kitchen, sitting at the table drinking tea.

"I told him he could stay," I inform her.

Mrs. Reynolds gives me a small smile. "I'm proud of you."

"I'm not."

"You'll get over it," she says. "You ready to plant more bulbs today?"

I pull old, worn overalls out of my backpack so I can spare myself from having to wear the muumuu.

Caleb's back is to me when I walk outside. Good. I take a bag of bulbs and slowly, carefully sit on the grass. With a small shovel in hand, I start digging.

"Don't forget, Margaret. Six inches deep," Mrs. Reynolds says from behind, leaning over me to inspect my work.

"Got it, six inches."

"And make sure you place the bulbs right-side up."

"Okay," I say.

"And scatter them. Don't place them in a pattern or else it looks funny."

The old lady takes a lawn chair and places it right next to me so she can oversee my work.

"Why don't you supervise him?" I ask, pointing to where Caleb has taken panels of wood and seems to be attempting to put them in some kind of order.

"He's doing just fine. Besides, I don't know the first thing about building a gazebo."

I dig three holes, carefully make soft soil pillows for them, then place the bulbs into the holes and scoot myself down to plant more. After a while Mrs. Reynolds falls asleep in the chair. She usually does this at least once a day, and when I tell her she dozed off for an hour, she totally denies it. I'm surprised she can sleep with all the hammering Caleb's doing, but the lady hears, as she more often than not admits, like the dead.

I glance up at Caleb. He's a fast worker, already starting to nail planks together as if he builds gazebos every day. His shirt is soaking wet from sweat in his armpits, chest, and back. And it obviously doesn't bother him that one of my conditions is that we ignore each other. He does an incredible job of ignoring me. I don't think he's even glanced in my direction once.

But now he stops hammering, his back still to me when he yells, "Would you stop staring at me?"

TWENTY-THREE

Caleb

You ignore me, and I'll ignore you. Maggie, like every other girl in my life, is trying to control me. I'm sick of the games, I'm sick of feeling like a jerk. And most of all I'm sick of people gawking at me because I went to jail.

I know she's staring at me, I can feel her eyes on me like little pin pricks poking into my back. Out of frustration, I pound the next nail into the two-by-four harder than I normally would and whack my forefinger with the hammer.

I glare at Maggie.

The girl is sitting on the ground wearing torn and stained overalls. "I . . . I wasn't staring at you," she stutters.

"The hell you weren't," I bark back. I hold my arms

out wide. "You want to gawk at the ex-con, you got it. Just answer one thing for me, will ya? You like it when people stare at *you* when you limp around like you're gonna topple over any second?"

Maggie sucks in a breath, then covers her nose and mouth with her hand as she hobbles inside the house.

Oh crap.

My finger is throbbing, my head is pounding, and I insulted a crippled girl—a girl I'm responsible for crippling. I should just go to hell right now because the deal with the devil is probably signed anyway.

Mrs. Reynolds has no clue what's happening, her head is slumped in the chair and she's snoring.

I throw down the hammer and go into the house to find Maggie. I hear sniffling sounds coming from the kitchen. Maggie is standing at the counter, taking vegetables out of the refrigerator. She pulls out a cutting board and starts cutting them with a huge butcher knife.

"I'm sorry," I say. "I shouldn't have said that."

"It's fine."

"Obviously it's not or you wouldn't be crying."

"I'm not crying."

I lean my hip against the counter. "There's tears running down your face." Plain as day I can see 'em.

She picks up an onion and holds it out to me. "My eyes tear when I cut onions."

My fists clench together, because I can't shake her and

make her yell at me. This time I deserve to be yelled at. "Say something."

Instead of responding, she chops the onion in two. I imagine she's pretending that onion is my head . . . or some other part of my body.

"Fine, have it your way," I say, then leave her. If she wants to live in silence, that's her choice.

I clench my teeth so much they hurt, and the rest of the afternoon I work outside on the gazebo. It feels good to create something useful, something to finally make someone proud of me for a change. Because the rest of my life I've totally fucked up.

Maggie abandoned her post in the yard. She hasn't been outside since I went off on her.

At seven I inform a waking Mrs. Reynolds I'm leaving for the day and head for the bus stop. Maggie's not far behind.

I'm standing on the corner of Jarvis and Lake Streets, backpack flung over my shoulder, when a car screeches beside me.

"What are you doing slumming on this side of town, rich boy?"

Oh, man. It's Vic Medonia. And some other guys on the Fremont High wrestling team.

"None of your fucking business," I say.

Vic laughs, bitterness dripping off the cackling sound. "Your friends in jail taught you how to stand on the street corner and pimp yourself? How much you charging for that used booty of yours, anyway?"

The other guys in the car laugh, then Vic gets out. He looks to my right and says, "Is this your new girlfriend?"

I turn to see Maggie not far away, limping toward us as she heads for the bus stop.

"Maggie, go back to the house," I warn her. I've seen enough fights to know that Vic is looking for one. Hoping to redirect Vic, I say, "This is between you and me, man. Leave her out of it."

Vic laughs, the high pitched sound making my skin crawl. "Check her out, guys. Jeez, Becker, you really are scraping the bottom of the barrel. Does it turn you on when she struts around like a retard like that?"

I drop my backpack and charge him. We both land on the ground, but one of his friends grabs me from behind and pins my hands back. Before I can free my arms, Vic clocks me right on the jaw and the ribs.

Before I know what's happening, Maggie is in the middle of us, swinging her book bag and hitting Vic. The chick has more in her than she lets on.

Through all the commotion, I break free and push the prick who'd been holding me, then I grab Maggie and act as her shield before she gets herself killed. "Run," I order her as I tackle one of the guys.

I'm punching and grasping at shirt collars as much as I can in a three-against-one fight. Odds are against me and it's not a pretty sight. All mayhem freezes when I hear a siren, attached to a cruiser with red and blue lights flashing. An officer flies out of the car and has us kneel on the ground with our hands over our heads. "What's going on here, boys?"

I don't see Maggie.

"Nothing," Vic says. "We were just playing around. Right, Becker?"

I stare straight at Vic and say, "Right."

"Doesn't look like nothing to me." The cop holds his hand out to me, palm up. "Let me see some ID."

Since my driver's license was revoked, I only have my community service ID tag from the DOC. I'm not about to pull it out and have him call Damon. I'll be locked up again before you can say "hit-and-run."

"I don't have any," I say.

"What are you doing in Hampton?"

"Visiting a friend."

The guy does a great cop stance from the movies, with his feet apart and his hands on his hips positioned right above his gun belt. "Let me give you a piece of advice. We don't take kindly to strangers coming into our town and causing trouble." He turns to Vic. "I suggest you meet your friend on his turf or I'll have to get your parents involved. Got it?"

This should be about the time I tell the cop the truth: that I'm in Hampton by the order of the Illinois Juvenile Department of Corrections. But I won't.

"Got it," Vic says.

The officer gets back in his squad car and orders Vic

and his friends to move on. He follows Vic's car. I watch until both cars are out of sight.

When I look around for my backpack, I quickly realize it's gone. One of Vic's friends probably snatched it. But that's the least of my worries.

My jaw is starting to protest Vic's punch, and I put my hand up to my face to feel if it's bleeding. When I do, Maggie reveals herself.

Our eyes lock.

The bus to Paradise comes rumbling down the street and we both get on it. I sit at my usual spot in back and she follows, sitting right next to me. I'm surprised until I notice her fingers shaking.

She's scared.

It's demented and strange after all that's happened, but she feels safe with me right now. I don't dare touch her, 'cause that would mean this is something more than it is. And I know this . . . this feeling of friendship is a fleeting, temporary thing. What scares me to fucking death is that some part of my brain has decided this insignificant act of Maggie sitting next to me is the first step in fixing all that's gone wrong in my life.

Which makes it all the more significant.

TWENTY-FOUR

Maggie

I saw Caleb today at school. Rumors are running rampant about the bruises on his face.

None of the rumors are true.

After school I get on the bus to go to Mrs. Reynolds' house. I walk down the aisle to where Caleb is sitting. He doesn't look up. I take the seat next to him like I did yesterday.

This time he doesn't walk behind me after we're dropped off at the bus stop by Mrs. Reynolds' house. We walk side by side, as if there's an unspoken understanding between the two of us. I'm the only one (besides Vic and his thug friends) who knows how Caleb got his bruises. The fight yesterday scared me. Did Caleb get caught up in the fight because Vic insulted me? Whatever the reasons were, it was us against them. Caleb and I were on the same team and we didn't have a chance of winning.

That's why I ran behind a tree and called 911 from my cell, to protect him/us, because he would never be able to fight off three guys by himself, and God knows my cheap book bag couldn't take much more. I've never been able to stomach a fight anyway. The fight is over, but its aftereffects have lingered.

So now it's another day at Mrs. Reynolds' house working together, but not.

Caleb still follows my conditions: he doesn't talk to me as he works on the gazebo and I plant more daffodils.

I hum songs as I work. Sometimes Mrs. Reynolds hums along with me, until she starts belting out words to the songs so loud that I stop working and blink my eyes at this old lady who doesn't care what people think about her. It's really mind-boggling.

When Mrs. Reynolds starts nodding off, I walk inside the house and pour myself a glass of water. Before I leave the kitchen, I pour one for Caleb too. Quietly, I set it down on one of the wooden planks beside him.

Heading back inside to prepare a small snack, I remember I forgot to bring the cookie plate down from the attic last week. I go up the two flights of stairs to the attic and pick up the plate.

The door closes and I shriek. Caleb is standing in the attic with me, the glass of water in his hand. "Oh my God!"

"I'm not going to hurt you, Maggie. I just wanted to say thanks for the water and . . . well, and I know it's not easy working together, but I do appreciate you not kicking me out."

"You can't leave," I say.

"Why not?"

"Because that door locks automatically."

Caleb eyes the door stopper he just kicked out of the way. "You're joking, right?"

I shake my head slowly. I'm trying not to panic at the reality of being stuck with Caleb Becker in an attic. *Breathe, Maggie.* In. Out. In. Out.

Caleb tries turning the knob, then tries a turn-door-knob-while-pushing-on-door action. "Shit." He turns to me. "You and me. In the same room. This is *not* supposed to happen."

"I know," I say.

"We could yell for Mrs. Reynolds. She's sleeping outside, but—"

"She'll never hear us all the way out there. Her hearing is marginal if you're ten feet away. When she wakes up we'll hear her and then yell our heads off."

"So you're saying we're stuck here?"

I nod again.

"Shit."

"You already said that," I inform him.

Caleb starts pacing while running his hands over his buzz cut. "Yeah, well, this sucks. Being locked up is getting to be the theme of my life," he mumbles. "How long before she usually wakes up?"

I shrug. "It could be a half hour, but sometimes she sleeps for an hour or more, like yesterday."

Taking a deep breath, he sits in the middle of the floor and leans against Mrs. Reynolds' trunk. "You might as well take a seat," he says.

"I'm kind of afraid of spiders."

"Still?"

"You remember that about me?"

"How could I forget? You and Leah used to make me your personal spider killer," he says.

I look at him strangely.

"Sit," he orders. "I'm giving the old lady two hours to free us and then I'm breaking that door down."

Neither of us say anything for a long time. The only sound is our breathing and the eerie bangs and creaks of the old house.

"Was it scary in jail?" I ask, breaking the silence.

"Sometimes."

"Like when? What did they do to you?"

I turn and look at him. His expression is wary. "You know, you're the first one who's asked for details."

"I'll admit I've heard the rumors. I suspect most of them aren't true."

"What'd you hear?"

I curl my lip, nervous to be the one to tell him. "Let's see . . . you had a boyfriend in jail . . . you joined a gang . . . you attempted to escape and got solitary confinement . . . you beat up a guy who afterward needed to be hospitalized . . . should I continue?"

"You believe any of it?"

"No. Why? Are they true?"

He leans his head back against the trunk and lets out a long breath. "I was in a fight and got thrown in solitary for it." He puts his palms over his eyes. "I was in solitary for thirty-six hours. God, I can't believe I'm talking to you, of all people, about this."

"Did they give you food and water?"

He laughs. "Yeah, you still get meals. But you're sleeping on a slab of cement and a one-inch foam mattress on top of that. A stainless steel toilet is your only companion."

"At least you were alone," I say. "I had to wait for someone to bring a plastic bowl for me to go to the bathroom while I was in the hospital. Then I had to lay there while they wiped me. It was so degrading."

"Do the doctors say you'll ever walk without a limp?"

"They don't know. I have to go to physical therapy twice a week until I go to Spain."

"Spain?"

I explain why I'm working at Mrs. Reynolds' house every day and about my dream of leaving Paradise so I can get away from the past.

"I couldn't wait to get back home," he admits. "Coming back here meant I was free of being locked up."

"That's because you're Caleb Becker. People will always

accept you. The only thing that kept me from being a loser before was tennis and Leah. Now that I've lost both, I have nothing except humiliating stares and comments people say but don't think I hear."

Caleb stands and paces the attic again. "Coming home has sucked. But leaving Paradise would be a copout."

"To me," I tell him, "leaving Paradise means freedom. I feel locked up just living in this town where everybody reminds me what a loser I am now."

Caleb crouches down, his face right in front of mine. "You are *not* a loser. Hell, Maggie, you always knew what you wanted and went for it."

I tell him the honest truth. "Not anymore. When you hit me, a part of me died."

TWENTY—FIVE

Caleb

"Caleb, phone!" Mom yells from the kitchen.

I've been in my room, trying to figure out these mixed-up thoughts I've been having since Tuesday, when Maggie and I got locked in the attic. We sat there for maybe forty minutes. In that short amount of time I probably shared more with her than I have with Kendra. Ever.

I'm in serious trouble here.

I pick up the cordless and head to my room. "Hello?"

"Hey, CB. It's Brian."

"What's up?"

"It's Sunday," Brian says in a way-too-cheery tone.

"And?" I say.

"Come on, dude, don't tell me you forgot our ritual. You, me, Drew, and Tristan . . ."

I remember. Sunday afternoons watching football— me, Brian, Tristan, and Drew. *No chicks allowed* was our motto.

"I'm leaving for Tristan's in ten. Be ready," Brian says, then the line goes dead.

I'm in my briefs. I'd sworn to myself I'd sleep all day. But if I want to get back into a normal routine, Sunday football can't be ignored.

I take a quick shower—believe me I'm used to them. And when I'm pulling on some old sweats and a t-shirt, I hear Mom downstairs fawning over Brian.

I'm so glad you called Caleb. You're such a good friend. Here's some leftover Chinese food from last night. I swear she's like an out-of-control machine.

When I get downstairs, Brian says to me, "Your mom rocks, CB. Check out all the stuff she packed for us."

I glance into the large grocery bag. Mom must have put half of the food from our refrigerator in it. I'm about to hug her, but she picks up a dish rag and starts wiping off the kitchen table when I come close. "Go on," she says, "and have a good time."

At Tristan's house we have to wait for the game to come on. It's the Packers against the Bears. Before I got arrested, I could have told you every date of every game and every Bears' opponent playing in those games.

I park myself on the couch in his basement and lean

back. I can hardly wait to watch. The other guys have no clue how much I missed this.

Hell, I didn't even realize how much I missed this.

I got Kendra back, I got my friends back. I've got to forget about Maggie. I'm sure I'm just thinking about her so much because we're working together. I came back to Paradise with a mission to get my life back to normal. Sitting back and watching the game makes me realize that the status quo isn't all that bad.

Until Tristan starts tossing cans of Michelob to each of us.

"Where'd you get the brew?" Drew asks.

"From the Fourth of July. I snatched a case from my parents' party and hid it. My mom didn't even know it was missing."

"Way to go, man," Brian says. "Toss one of those puppies over here."

Brian and Drew catch theirs and open them right away. I catch the one thrown to me. Tristan holds his can up. "To a new season of Bears ball."

"To a quarterback who can actually throw the ball," Brian says.

"And a running back that can actually run the ball," Drew offers.

They all turn to me, waiting for my dumb football wisdom.

I'm holding the can, the coldness against my palm sending a chill up my arm. "And a punter who could kick the ball," I add, wondering if they realize I haven't flipped the top and opened it yet.

They all take a swig. Except me. I may have jeopardized going back to jail when I got in a fight with Vic when he insulted Maggie, but that was worth the risk. I haven't even been near alcohol since the night of the accident. I'm not about to jeopardize going back for a stupid can of beer.

"What do you think you're doing?" an adult voice from the staircase calls out.

Shit, it's Tristan's mom.

I would try to hide the beer, but that'd be pointless. We've already been busted.

She storms down the stairs and rips the Michelob out of Tristan's hand. "Not in my house, you won't," she says, then points her finger at me. "You may think you can just come back here and suck everyone into your lifestyle, Caleb, but I won't let that happen."

Tristan steps forward. "Ma, stop."

"Don't protect him, Tristan." She looks down at the beer can in my hand, then shakes her head in disgust. "Caleb, please leave my house."

I put the unopened can down on the table. Mrs. Norris doesn't even look at the can. She's too busy staring at me and sneering. "Stay away from my son," she orders as I head out.

There's no use even defending myself. Mrs. Norris already has her mind made up about me. Verdict: Guilty.

Besides, if I explain the truth she won't believe me. The way she glared at me says more than words ever will.

"That was a buzz kill," Brian says when we're back in his car. "Where are we gonna watch the game now? It's probably close to halftime."

"We can go back to my place," I offer.

Ten minutes later we settle ourselves in my basement and watch the game. The Bears are up by three, but the Packers have the ball and it's the fourth quarter.

I'm totally into the game when Brian says, "I need to tell you something."

"Shoot," I say, taking a handful of potato chips and shoving them into my mouth. My attention is still on the game, but I chance a small glance at my friend.

Brian is leaning forward, the expression on his face totally serious. "She'll kill me for telling you."

I glance back at the TV. The Packers just fumbled and it's the Bears' ball. This could clinch a victory for them. "Who?" I say, only partially listening to Brian.

"Kendra."

Kendra was recently in my arms and a willing partner in my bed. It wasn't the most romantic reunion; I guess I expected it to be like old times. It's been anything but.

"Did you see that?" I ask Brian, getting totally riled about the Bears game. You can't blame me for being excited when I'd been restricted from watching football for the past year. I missed a whole season. "They just sacked Edmonton!"

"We're together, CB. I just thought you should know."

I look at him, confused. "What the hell are you talking about?"

"Me . . . and Kendra."

It hits me like a brick smacked into my head at lightning speed. "*You* and Kendra?"

"Yeah."

Jeez. The word comes out of my mouth faster than my brain can comprehend it. "When?"

"You don't want to know."

That means it was before I was arrested. Maggie wasn't lying to me that night I freaked out on her.

Maggie had told me the truth while Kendra looked me right in the eye, feeding me lies. Kendra was the manipulative one and I fell for it.

But it all makes sense now, why Kendra is desperate to keep our relationship a secret. Perfect time to fuck with my head once again.

Brian is watching me, gauging my reaction. There's no way in hell I'm going to tell him I've been messing around with Kendra.

In a matter of seconds, I lose my demented perception of reality. There is no getting back together with Kendra, there is no hanging out with the guys like before. My life now has no resemblance to before. How could I ever have thought it had?

I have to ask. "Are you guys, you know . . ."

"Yeah."

I close my eyes and lean back into the cushions of the couch. Wow. My girlfriend was screwing both of us and I was oblivious. But Maggie knew and tried to warn me. As a thank-you, I insulted her and then the night spun out of control, ending up with Maggie in the hospital.

The Bears game forgotten, I shake my head and stare at the ceiling.

"At first it was just a hook-up, a mistake," Brian continues. "We both didn't mean for it to happen."

I wish Brian would just shut up. Now I know what Damon means about taking the blame. "You were probably so stoked I was convicted, you could finally have my girlfriend all to yourself," I say.

"It's not like that." Brian pauses. "I love her, Caleb. Jesus, I'd marry her right now if I could."

"Damn," I mumble. I wonder who's going to be there when Brian comes back from la-la land and falls flat on his face. Kendra told me there were no guys that mattered. Or was that all bullshit, too?

"She made me promise not to tell you about us. But I think it's cool if we're all up front about it, don't you? Then we can be a couple at school again, instead of pretending we're not together."

I stand, needing some distance. This is my best friend from when I was in kindergarten. I remember when Drew took a crayon away from Brian in first grade and I pinched Drew on the arm in retaliation.

And when I had chicken pox in sixth grade and had

to stay home for over a week from school, Brian secretly came over and played Dungeons & Dragons with me. And we never told our parents, even when Brian got stuck with the pox two weeks later.

I'd never thought Brian would betray our friendship.

"You're a prick," I blurt out.

Brian stands and grabs his car keys. "I knew you wouldn't understand. That's why I didn't tell you."

"Dude, you were screwing my girl behind my back. How'd you think I'd react?" A shiver just ran up and down my spine when I actually put the truth into words.

"I thought you'd listen. And try to understand without wanting to rip my head off. This is real, Caleb."

I give a cynical laugh. "I'll tell you what's real. Real is that I was in jail for the past year, rooming with drug dealers and eating crap food your dog wouldn't touch. Real is not being able to wear your own frickin' underwear and showering with twenty-five other dicks every day while guards watch. Real is my next-door neighbor who walks like she's balancing on stilts because her leg is so fucked up from the accident. Brian, your perception of reality is totally off."

Brian heads for the stairs, his back stiff. He stops when he's halfway up. "When you want to forgive me and move on, you know where I am."

My fists are clenched so tight they're getting numb.

That's when Mom walks down the stairs. She smiles wide and says in a cheery voice, "Did you have fun with your friends?"

TWENTY-SIX

Maggie

I wish my mom didn't insist on going to my physical therapy appointment.

"You can just drop me off," I say. "Just come back and get me in an hour."

Mom shakes her head. "Dr. Gerrard wants to talk with both of us."

Oh, no. "Mom, I'm fine. Robert expects his patients to do the impossible, that's all."

"I know it's not easy, Maggie," she says. "Don't worry, you don't have to do what feels uncomfortable. Just do your best."

When we enter the hospital, sure enough Robert is waiting for us. "Hi, Maggie, how we doing today?"

We? "Fine."

"Been doing those strengthening exercises I taught you?"

Uh . . . "Yeah. Well, sometimes."

Robert shakes my mom's hand. "Nice to see you again, Mrs. Armstrong."

"You too," she responds, then takes a seat while Robert leads me to the workout mat.

"Let's start with stretching," Robert says. "And warm up those muscles to help them work hard. Put your legs in a V."

I do, but my legs resemble an "I" more than a "V" because my left leg doesn't want to warm up right now. It's not me, it's the leg.

"That's the best you can do?"

"I think so."

Robert kneels beside me and says, "Touch your left foot with your left hand."

I try, but I only get as far as my knee.

"Come on, Maggie. A couple more inches."

I reach about another half inch, which doesn't impress my physical therapist.

"She can't," my mom interjects. "Can't you see she's in pain?"

"Mrs. Armstrong," Robert says. "Maggie has to push herself in order to retrain those muscles."

Mom is about to respond when Dr. Gerrard walks in. "Hello ladies. Robert."

My mom stands and hugs my surgeon. After the accident,

he was the one who always gave us hope and had the hands to reconstruct the inside of my leg. I remember the first time I met him in the hospital. He came in with a big white coat, a big smile, and big fingers that were going to cut my leg open and fix it.

Dr. Gerrard kneels next to me. "How's it going, Maggie? Run any marathons lately?"

I raise my eyebrows.

"I'm just kidding," he admits. "Bad surgeon joke."

"Dr. Gerrard, you need new material," I mumble.

"That's what my interns say, too." Dr. Gerrard has me sit on the examining table and inspects my scars. "Looks good," he says, then looks up. "Robert tells me you're a little timid in physical therapy."

Robert stands there with his clipboard in his hands, the traitor.

I shrug. "I can't put a lot of pressure on my foot."

"It hurts her," Mom chimes in.

My doctor steps back and takes a deep breath. "Okay, walk to the door and back for me, Maggie."

He helps me off the table while I limp to the door.

"Can you put more pressure on your left foot?"

"Not really."

"Okay, come back and sit down."

I limp back to the table and sit on it. Mom comes up to me and rubs my back.

"I'm going to give it to you straight," Dr. Gerrard says.

"You've got to start pushing yourself and stop favoring your left side."

"I'm doing my best," I say.

Dr. Gerrard doesn't accuse me of lying, but I can tell he's not convinced by the way he's pursing his lips together.

"Maybe we should let up on the physical therapy," my mom says.

Dr. Gerrard sucks air into his clenched teeth, the hissing sound clearly a no-go to Mom's suggestion. "I'd hate to see her stop physical therapy."

"I have a suggestion," Robert pipes in. "What if Maggie starts playing tennis again?"

My heart pumps faster, the beats within my body thumping in my chest like an Indian tribal dance.

"Are you okay?" Mom asks.

I can't answer. My esophagus feels like it's constricting.

"I need to get some air," I say, then get off the table.

Robert comes up to me. "Maggie, we're just trying to help you."

"I know. But I can't do this anymore. I just can't." I pull on my sweats, limp past my mom, and head for the exit. I'm passing people in wheelchairs, doctors, and nurses. Do they think I'm as crazy as I feel?

When the doors open I suck in fresh air and try to breathe deeply.

Breathe. In. Out. In. Out.

Isn't breathing supposed to be something you do unconsciously? Right now I'm hyperconscious about it. So conscious, in fact, that I think if I stop concentrating, I might just forget to do it. I close my eyes.

Breathe. In. Out. In. Out.

I felt this way the day my dad left the last time, when I realized it might be his last visit. I wasn't strong then, either.

I blink back tears as I try hard to forget. Because it hurts too much knowing his love for me wasn't strong enough to make him stay. I wasn't worth being loved enough.

Tennis was my saving grace, but even that didn't work. I deserved to be admired on the court, because I was worth something when I played. Not only was I part of the team, I was the one my teammates looked up to.

The more that other dads showed up to matches, the harder I would play. It was as if I wanted those dads to regret I wasn't their kid. No matter if my dad loved me or not, there would be other dads that would do anything to have me be their daughter. Having other dads congratulate me was worth more to me than the varsity trophy I earned my sophomore year. I might not be worthy of my dad's love, but I was worthy of that trophy.

A pain in my leg shoots up into my spine, a mocking reminder that I'll never be a champion again.

"Maggie?"

I turn toward my mom, who's now officially freaked out.

"I can't play tennis," I tell her.

"Dr. Gerrard wants you to try. You will try, won't you?"

But I won't be good, and then my dad won't have any-

thing to be proud of me for. He'll never want me to be part of his new family. "Can we go home? I want to go home."

Mom sighs. I hate feeling like I'm disappointing her. I know she tries so hard to support us emotionally, physically, and financially. She's like the little cheerleader of our family.

When we get in the car, I calm down. I look at my mom, driving the car with a sad look on her face. "Mom, what do you want out of life?"

She gives a little laugh. "Right now, money."

"Besides money."

She cocks her head to the side, thinking. When we reach a red light, she turns to me. "I guess I'd like a partner to share my life with."

"Do you miss Dad?"

"Sometimes. I miss the companionship, I miss going out as a couple. I don't miss the fights."

The light turns green and we accelerate, our car passing a woman and man holding hands with their daughter. "Will he ever want me to visit him?"

"One day," she says, but I can tell she's not so sure.

"Do you want to date Mr. Reynolds?" I ask.

Her eyes go wide. "Why would you ask such a thing?"

"Because you were dancing with him at the Fall Festival. He doesn't have kids. I think he came to be with you."

Mom laughs, this big laugh that fills the car, and the people in the next car could probably hear her, too.

"Auntie Mae's Diner was a sponsor of the event, Maggie. That's why Lou was there."

"Well," I say defensively, "you two were looking pretty chummy."

"He was just being nice."

I shake my head. "I don't think so."

"Hmm . . ."

"What does that mean?"

"Nothing. Just go back to being a kid, will ya?"

We sit in silence the rest of the way home. When we walk inside the house, I ignore the lump in my throat as I say, "For the record . . . if you want to invite Mr. Reynolds over for dinner one night, I wouldn't mind," and head upstairs to my room.

In my room, I want to take my words back. I only said them because I know how miserable Mom has been lately.

But the truth is I miss my dad every day, too. More than anything. And I know he has another wife and another life. What if Mom and Mr. Reynolds start dating or, even worse, get married. Will they want to start a new life without me, too?

I lock my door and open my closet. In the back, in the darkest shadows, is my racquet. I know it's there although it's hidden behind clothes. I feel its presence when I'm in my room, kind of like kryptonite for Superman. Desperation washes over me.

I reach out and grab the handle, the weight of the racquet foreign but, at the same time, familiar.

"Maggie, open the door."

Panic. "Just a second."

I toss the racquet in the closet and unlock my door. Mom is staring at me strangely.

I brush the hair from my face, hoping she can't see right through me and realize I've always known where my lost racquet is. "Mom, what's up?"

"I was thinking. About Lou, my boss. Were you serious when you said I should invite him for dinner?"

TWENTY–SEVEN

Caleb

I asked Brian to meet me at the park for some one-on-one. I'm practicing free throws when he drives up in his Yukon.

"You look like a middle-aged man in that thing," I say.

He gives a fake-insulted huff. "It's better than the car you drive."

"I don't drive one."

"Exactly."

We stand facing each other. I say what needs to be said. "Listen, about you and Kendra. How about we call a truce."

"Fair enough."

I pass him the ball. He dribbles the ball too far away from his body, so I knock it and grab it away from him.

"B-ball's still not your game, is it?" I say as I dribble down the court.

Brian's shuffling backwards, following my every move. When I stop, his hands are up and ready to block my shot. "Get me on a wrestling mat and I'll kick your ass."

I take a shot. It bounces off the rim and Brian gets the rebound.

Brian is an anxious player. He runs down the court and shoots too quickly, missing the basket by a mile. The ball lands in the grass. I take the ball inbounds. "You're a lightweight, Bri," I say. "I'd pin you in less than ten seconds."

"Put your money where your mouth is, big guy, tomorrow after school."

I move around Brian and make an easy lay-up. "I have to work."

He holds the ball. "You say that, but you never say where. Rumor has it you're a homo and meet up with your lover after school. Is he the one who gave you the bruise on your face?"

My muscles start to tense up. "Don't give me shit."

Brian starts dribbling down the court, his eye on the basket. "Why? You gonna threaten me like you threatened Drew?"

Brian shoots and the ball goes right in.

This time I hold the ball under my arm, stopping the game. "He was trying to piss me off and you know it."

My old friend crosses his arms on his chest. "You've

changed, Caleb. I don't even know you anymore. And this has nothing to do with Kendra."

"Bullshit. I'm the same person."

He laughs. "You've got a chip on your shoulder. Everybody knows it but you. That's the scary part."

No, the scary part is that people don't realize how much *they've* changed. "So everyone else is the same except me?"

"No, dude. *Everybody's* changed, nobody is the same. You're the only one who can't accept it. You're not a sophomore anymore, you're not dating Kendra, you're not the wrestling stud. You're a bad-ass, brooding ex-con."

I'll show him a brooding ex-con. I dribble the ball down the court, and when Brian gets in my face I push him down before I take the shot.

"Foul!" Brian calls out.

"You said to accept my bad-ass ex-con self. I'm only taking your suggestion."

I hold out a hand. He looks at me suspiciously, then grabs my wrist as I pull him up. I get three more baskets and recover two of Brian's rebounds.

"You know what you need?" Brian says as he wipes sweat from his brow.

"A new best friend?" I suggest.

"No. You need a girlfriend. Name a chick you think is hot. Just throw out a name."

"Maggie Armstrong."

"No, seriously. Name a chick."

"I am serious."

"Dude, that's sick. You went to jail because of her."

"I'm well aware of that."

"You're telling me you have the hots for *the* Maggie Armstrong? Your next-door neighbor? The girl who walks weird because you ran over her leg with your car?"

"Brian, you're starting to act like Drew."

Brian looks confused as he's trying to comprehend what I just admitted to him. Then he bursts out laughing. He can't stop and falls to the ground in hysterics, holding his stomach. "That's . . . *hilarious!*" he yells when he can catch his breath. "Oh my God, it *can't* be true . . ." he says, then goes back to laughing hysterically again.

I'm seriously considering kicking his ass right now. But this isn't Vic or Drew, this is Brian. I take the ball and head back home, but not before telling Brian to go to hell.

Nobody is home; I have the house all to myself. I want to yell at the top of my lungs, but just as I'm about to do it the doorbell rings. Brian is an idiot if he's stupid enough to come here to laugh in my face again. Maybe, after all, I will use his head as my punching bag.

But I open the door and my ex-best friend isn't standing in front of me. It's Kendra, my ex-girlfriend. Shiny lips and all. "Hi," she says.

"Hi."

"Are your parents home?"

"Nope." She already knew they weren't.

"Can I come in?"

I open the door wider. She heads straight upstairs to my room. I watch her back and my eyes focus on her thong underwear sticking out of the top of her shorts before I follow.

Closing my door like I always do when we're about to fool around, I lean back against the door and watch her. But this time we're not going to fool around. I know it. She doesn't, obviously, I can tell by what she's wearing. A ridiculously low-cut shirt, I swear her nipples are millimeters below the ruffled collar. And her shorts reveal way more than I'd ever want any girlfriend of mine to reveal. But she's not my girlfriend, she's Brian's.

Kendra wanders around my bedroom, fingering my desk, my dresser, and my bookshelves. When she picks up my lightsaber and turns it on, I'm tempted to tell her not to touch it.

"When are you going to get rid of these toys?" she asks, waving it in the air.

I don't answer.

Sighing, she says, "I know Brian told you about him and me. But I still love you, you know." She closes the distance between us, close enough that I can smell her cherry lips. She licks them and leans in for a kiss.

I turn my head away. "What? One boyfriend isn't enough for you?"

"I want you both."

"It's over, Kend. Way over."

"It's not and you know it. Because—and I know this

sounds selfish, but it's true—I don't want anyone else to have you."

"Break up with Brian. The guy wants to marry you."

She chuckles. "My parents think he's good for me, so I'm playing along. Besides, I need a boyfriend I can hang with in public. But you can be my private boyfriend, CB."

"Never gonna happen."

"Wanna bet?" She steps back, points the tip of the saber at me, and pushes the blunt tip against my throat. A wicked grin crosses her mouth. "You can be my little secret. You like keeping secrets, don't you Caleb?"

My pulse quickens, and the mood in the room changes instantly. One thought burns in my brain . . . *she knows*.

"What do you want?" I say evenly.

"CB, don't look so sad. I just want you," she says, then lowers the saber and goes in for another kiss.

This time I don't turn away.

TWENTY-EIGHT
Maggie

It took a week for Mom to invite Mr. Reynolds over for
dinner. She asked me about twenty more times if it was
okay with me. I didn't have the heart to say no.

Mr. Reynolds comes in the house wearing a grey three-
piece suit and red tie, as if he's going to court for a traffic
violation. In his hands are a dozen purple tulips for my
mom and a box of Frango chocolates for me.

"Thanks," I say awkwardly as he hands me the box.
Do I open it now, or wait until later . . . or tomorrow?

"Why don't you have a seat and make yourself comfortable, Lou," Mom says nervously, her hands fidgeting with
the black, sophisticated dress she decided to wear. "Would
you like a drink? Wine . . . brandy . . . soft drink?"

Mr. Reynolds smiles, a warm smile that I can tell is sincere. "Surprise me."

Mom laughs, a sweet, soft laugh I haven't heard in years.

When Mom is in the kitchen, Mr. Reynolds turns to me. "How is it back at school after being away for a year?"

I shrug. "It's okay, I guess."

He stares out the window. Where's my mom? The clock on the fireplace mantle is ticking, each second a reminder of how time is passing so slowly.

Tick. Tick. Tick.

Mr. Reynolds rubs his hands together. I can tell he's as eager as I am for my mom to come back.

Tick. Tick. Tick.

I want to excuse myself and hide in my room. I don't think I can handle watching my mom on a date with someone other than my dad.

Just as I'm about to stand up and excuse myself, she comes in with three drinks and a big smile. "Martinis for us, Sprite for Maggie."

Mr. Reynolds takes the glass from my mom. Their hands touch slightly when she hands it to him. I know I encouraged her to invite Mr. Reynolds over, but he's too big, too blonde, and . . . and he's not my dad.

I stand up.

Mom looks at me, her expression wary. "Where are you going, sweetheart?"

"To my room. I forgot to call Danielle."

Mom has this puppy dog look on her face; I think she knows I'm lying.

In my room I open the top drawer of my desk. In an envelope I keep my dad's phone number. My hands are shaking as I dial his number.

It rings three times before he answers. "Jerry Armstrong here."

"Um . . . Dad?"

"Maggie, is that you?"

"Yeah."

"How's my little girl holding up?"

"Fine."

"And your leg? The last time we talked you were having a bit of trouble."

"It's better, I guess."

It feels good to talk to my dad. Hearing his familiar voice takes away the black cloud that always seems to hover over me. I don't want to tell him the truth about my leg because I only want to share good news. If I'm positive, then maybe he won't want to forget I'm his daughter.

"Great. And school?"

I swallow the reality and say as cheerfully as I can, "Perfect. I'm getting all As," I lie.

"Wow."

There's silence, but I don't want him to hang up. I feel desperate. He sounds enthusiastic, but I'm not sure.

"How's your mother doing?" he finally says, breaking the silence.

She's currently having a date with her boss in our living room. "She's fine."

"Glad to hear it. I miss you, sweetheart."

"I miss you, too. When can I see you?"

No matter how many times I promise myself I won't beg him, I fail. It's like something inside me snaps when I think he's going to end the conversation. I want to yell, *Aren't I good enough?* but I don't.

"Sometime soon, when business settles down."

The black cloud returns—I've heard those exact words before. Too many times.

"Maggie, can you do me a favor?"

I'm holding back tears as I say, "What?"

"Tell your mother I sent her a check last week. And to have her lawyer stop calling mine. It's costing me a fortune every time he calls, like a hundred and fifty an hour."

"I'll tell her."

Someone else is talking in the background and I can tell I'm losing his attention. "I have to take another call, sweetheart. I'm sorry, it's important. I'll call you soon."

"Okay. I love you, Dad."

"Love you too, Mags."

Click.

I swallow hard and lean my head back against the wall. As much as I tell myself not to, I'm crying. I'd love to throw myself onto my bed and sob into my pillow, but Mom'll probably hear me.

The phone rings, startling me. I'm still holding the

cordless in my hand. Could it be my dad calling back so soon? He always says he'll call but never does. Maybe he's changed. Maybe he realizes after hearing my voice he misses me so much he can't stand it anymore.

"Hello?" I say excitedly.

There's a hesitation on the line, then a female voice recording says, "This is High Spring Water Company reminding you that there's a special on our five-gallon water bottles for the month of October. If you'd like to order—"

I hang up the phone in the middle of the recording. God, I feel so alone. There's nobody in my life who remotely understands what I've been going through.

Except one person.

My fingers dial the Becker's number automatically before my brain can comprehend what I'm doing.

"Hello."

It's him—Caleb. I don't even know what to say.

"Maggie? I know it's you, we have caller ID."

I forgot about that. "Hi," I mumble.

"What's up?"

Tears come to my eyes. "I just . . . wanted to talk to you."

"Why are you crying? Are you hurt? Did you fall?"

I can't talk because I don't want him to know how weak I am . . . how much I need his friendship right now. God, all those years I thought I would die if he didn't love me as much as I loved him. But now I realize how stupid I was.

"If you don't answer me, I'm coming over whether

your mom's there or not." His voice is hard and command-
ing, and I know he means it.

"No, don't come over. Can you meet me at Paradise
Park in ten minutes?"

"I'll be there," he promises.

I take the sleeve of my shirt and wipe at my eyes.
"Caleb?"

"Yeah."

"Thanks."

I splash water on my eyes in the bathroom, tell my mom
that I'm going over to Danielle's, and head for the park.

Caleb walks up a minute later wearing jeans and a t-
shirt with a plain button-down shirt over it. He slows his
stride when he sees me and, without a word, pulls me into
an embrace.

Now I'm losing it, right into his shirt. I clutch onto
him as the sobs start and don't stop. I let it all out—my
mom's date, my dad's conversation, my confusion about
it all. Caleb doesn't laugh, he doesn't pull away, he doesn't
talk . . . he just lets me be me.

When I settle down, I lean back and witness the mess
I've made on his shirt. "I made your shirt all gross," I say
between sniffles.

"Forget the shirt. What's going on? I couldn't understand a word you mumbled into my chest."

Now I'm half laughing and half crying. He looks down
at my hand. I do, too. He slowly reaches out and takes my
fingers in his. God, how I dreamed of us holding hands all

those years ago. He'd take my hand in his and we'd walk down the street together. I look up at his eyes. Usually they're dark and brooding, but now I see a warmth there I'd never noticed before. He leads me to the old oak. We both sit down, then he leans back against the tree right next to me and lets go of my hand. "Okay, now talk."

It's easy because I don't have to look at him, I can just spurt out all the stuff that's going wrong in my life. I take a deep breath. I'm going to attempt to say it all without going into hysterics again. "My mom has a date over, her boss and Mrs. Reynolds' son. I think my mom likes him, but I don't know if I'm ready for her to start dating. I know it's selfish, but my dad has practically ignored me ever since the divorce. He's re-married, you know. And I think his wife wants a kid, as if he doesn't already have one. To top it off, my doctor said I should play tennis again, and every time I think about it my throat starts constricting and I have to remember to breathe . . . and then I call you because you're the only one I feel I can talk to. Which is ridiculous because it's *you*."

Caleb plays with a piece of grass he's plucked from the ground. "Do you think your mom would be happy with this boss guy?" he asks.

I think back to the way Mom laughed at the Fall Festival and how nervous she was tonight. "Yeah, I do. But that's the part that scares me. It's like ending a chapter in your life and starting over. A single mom, boyfriends . . . so much has changed."

"You're stressing too much about what might be. Do

something to take your mind off thinking about what might never happen."

"Like what?"

"Pick up a racquet."

"That's not funny," I say, already stressing and wanting to flee.

"I'm not trying to be funny, Maggie." I hear him sigh, a low breath that comes out slow. "Can I see your scars?"

Oh my God. "No." I shake my head feverishly while still staring at the ground. And I'm aware that my breathing just got heavier.

"Please don't freak out on me."

"I'm not."

"You are. I went to jail for doing something to you and I have no clue what it looks like."

I turn my head and I'm staring into his eyes, darker and more intense than I've ever seen them. "Why are you looking at me like that?"

"Do you remember the accident?" he asks, totally focused on my answer.

I shake my head.

"You remember nothing? Our conversation before the accident, me hitting you with the car? *Nothing at all?*"

"No. It's a big blank. I only know what people told me."

He blinks, then looks away. "We fought, you and I."

"About what?"

He gives a short, cynical laugh. "Kendra."

I'm trying to breathe evenly so I don't give him a hint

that I do remember. Every word he spat at me when I told him I loved him. It's the only part of that night that's crystal clear to me. The rest is stuck in a foggy haze. "I don't remember," I lie.

"You said she was cheating on me, that you saw her with some other guy but you wouldn't tell me who. You were right, you know," he says. "She was with Brian before I got put in jail." He's staring at me again, and this time I can't look away. "You also said you loved me."

I swallow, still mesmerized by his eyes. Those eyes that never gave me more than a glance a year ago are burning into mine. "I don't remember," I whisper.

"Maggie—" He takes my hand in his and places my palm against his cheek roughened with a day's worth of stubble. He turns his head and kisses the inner, sensitive part of my palm, his eyes holding my gaze. "I should have done this a year ago."

My heart flips over as he leans in and touches his lips to mine.

TWENTY-NINE
Caleb

I couldn't sleep last night, which is nothing new because every night is filled with restlessness.

But last night it wasn't nightmares of jail keeping me awake, or the night of the accident and what I could have done differently. I was reliving what happened a few hours ago. Kissing Maggie was the stupidest thing I've ever done. But, looking into her sad eyes and vulnerable face made me want her more than I've ever wanted anything in my life.

Last night real emotions were flying. Last night honesty was flying. It felt so raw.

As I'm getting ready for school, I think about our conversation after the kiss. She was nervous, I could tell by the shaking of those lips against mine. She'd closed her eyes and clutched at me as our lips met. I swear I've never been more turned on. When I leaned back, she had a worried look on her face as if I was going to give her a flunking grade on her kissing skills.

I can't believe that happened, she'd said.

I don't even know how I responded. All I remember is this feeling of stupidity washing over me, and wondering what the hell made me kiss a girl I should avoid getting close to at all costs. But being close to her felt so damn right, I couldn't resist her. We've been through so much, our lives are meshed and we're stuck in this web together. The sick thing is, I don't want to get out of it.

Maggie is frustrating, she's confused, she's angry . . . and she hums these ridiculous tunes when she's working at Mrs. Reynolds' house. You'd think I'd go nuts from it. I can't help that I like it when she blows her hair off of her face when she's working, or when she looks at Mrs. Reynolds sideways when she's insisting Maggie's planting her stupid bulbs wrong . . . and when she's not humming, I resist the urge to tell her to continue.

Get a grip, Caleb. After you kissed her she ran home as fast as she could.

Okay, so after I kissed her she left me at the tree wondering how I got myself into this mess. As much as I want Maggie, I can't have her. Maybe I should write a letter and slip it into her locker, apologizing for last night.

I sit down at my desk and pull out a sheet of paper.

Maggie,
   Sorry about last night.
   Caleb

I read it back to myself and it sounds idiotic. I crumple it up and start again.

Maggie,
   If I scared you last night, I'm sorry. It was a harmless kiss that didn't mean anything.
   Caleb

I crumple it up almost as soon as I sign my name. Because it did mean something. Kendra's kisses are more hollow to me than a flute. And, dammit, I'm not sorry I slipped up and got close to Maggie. I wanted to kiss her and I still want to kiss her. Okay, so I'd rather have her say something like *Let's try that again,* but I'd settle for her not running away. Getting a grip, I head to school early and try to forget Maggie and last night.

I trudge through my day until I get to computer class. Maggie is sitting in front, her eyes fixated on the screen in front of her. She doesn't even notice when I walk in. I expected to get some sign from her that everything is cool between us, but I get zilch.

Oh, yeah. I do get something—Kendra. She's been giving me her best seduction smiles all day, promising to fulfill all my fantasies. Little does she know my fantasies are consumed with a girl who refuses to look in my direction.

Lucky for me I manage to ditch Kendra and her overexposed cleavage all day.

I head to the bus after school, trying without much success not to be surprised if Maggie sits up front instead of next to me. I plunk myself down in back and catch sight of her pink t-shirt and faded jeans coming up the aisle. Her long hair covers the side of her face, as if shielding it from my gaze. She passes the front seats and heads to the rear, never looking up at me.

When she slides in beside me and the bus heads away from the school, I let out a breath. Being at school is stressing me out. The teachers stare, the kids stare . . . everybody stares at me except Maggie these days.

I look down at our knees, slightly touching. Jeans against jeans. Does she notice the heat transferring from her body to mine? Does she even realize what she's doing to me? I know, I know, I'm not a virgin and the slightest touch of a girl's knee is driving me insane. I don't even know what I'm feeling for Maggie, I just know that I'm *feeling*. It's something I've tried to avoid and deny until yesterday, when I held her in my arms while her tears spilled onto my shirt.

God, our knees touching isn't enough. I need more.

She's knotting her fingers together on her lap as if she doesn't know what to do with them. I want to touch her, but what if she pulls away like before? I've never been such a wuss with a girl in my life.

I bite my bottom lip as I slide my hand about a millionth of a millimeter closer to her hand.

She doesn't seem fazed so I move it closer. And closer.

When the tips of my fingers touch her wrist, she freezes. But she doesn't jerk her hand away. *God, her skin is so soft,* I think as my fingers trail a path from her wrist to her knuckles to her smooth, manicured nails.

I swear touching her like this is driving me nuts. It's more erotic, more intense than any other time with Kendra. I feel as awkward and inexperienced as a freshman again. I look up. Everyone else is oblivious to the intensity of emotions running rampant in the back of the public bus.

When I look back down at my hand covering hers, I'm grateful she hasn't come to her senses and pulled away. As if she knows my thoughts, we both turn our hands at the same time so our hands are palm against palm . . . finger against finger. Her hand is dwarfed against mine. It makes her seem more delicate and petite than I'd realized. I feel a need to protect her and be her champion should she ever need one.

With a slight shift of my hand, I lace my fingers through hers.

I'm holding hands.

With Maggie Armstrong.

I'm not even going to think about how wrong it is because it feels so right. She's avoided looking right at me, but now she turns her head and our eyes lock. God, how come I never noticed before how long her eyelashes were and how her brown eyes have specks of gold that sparkle when the sun shines on them?

The bus stops suddenly and I look out the window. It's our stop. She must have realized this because she pulls her hand away from mine and stands. I follow behind her, still reeling.

We get to Mrs. Reynolds' house. I can smell the scent of cookies invading us as we walk inside.

"Oh, I'm so glad you both are here," Mrs. Reynolds chants. "Come in the kitchen. I have . . ." The old lady cocks her head to the side, eyeing Maggie and me in her living room. "Is it hot outside?" she asks.

Maggie shakes her head while I say, "Not particularly."

"Then why are you both so flushed?" she asks, raising her eyebrows.

Oh, crap. While Maggie shrugs and heads to the kitchen, I inform the old lady, "I'm a guy. I don't flush."

"Uh huh," she says.

After eating the cookies, which she insists are her own secret Snickerdoodle recipe, I head outside. As I'm working, I steal glances at Maggie as she kneels on the ground and plants the bulbs with Mrs. Reynolds' verbal instructions never far behind.

When the old lady takes her nap, I listen to Maggie hum while I work on the gazebo. It's soothing. Her voice floats through the air as I work. But when the humming stops, I look around and Maggie isn't here. I head into the house.

I find her taking lemons out of the refrigerator. I watch as she cuts and squeezes them into a pitcher.

"Are you following me?" she asks, but doesn't meet my gaze.

"Yeah," I say.

"Why?"

"Honestly?"

She looks at me, her eyebrows raised.

I give her the only honest and true answer I have. "You're where I want to be."

THIRTY

Maggie

"Maggie!" Mrs. Reynolds' voice bellows through the house.

Caleb pulls back and gives me a helpless look. Then he says, "I guess that's my cue to get back to work," and walks out of the kitchen.

I'm standing here, holding a half a lemon in my hand. I'm speechless, I'm excited . . . I'm a wreck. *Caleb wants to be where I am.*

This is not some minor guy. This is CALEB BECKER, the boy who I'd dreamed about for what seems like my entire life. The boy who I used to watch from my window just to tide me over until the next time I'd be in the same room with him.

This is the boy who hit me with his car and left me in the street.

But when I look into his eyes, I can tell he's not the same Caleb Becker I used to know. The old Caleb only cared about himself. I never thought he observed or cared about the world around him. Has my heart started to forgive him?

I ran away last night because our kiss was perfect. Like I'd always dreamed our first kiss would be. Afraid that he wouldn't want to ever kiss me again, or laugh, or . . . something would change it from perfect to something less, I left.

When the bus drops us off on the corner by our houses, I ask Caleb if he wants to come over.

"Is your mom home?" he asks.

"Not for another hour."

He shrugs and says, "Sure."

I lead him into my house and up to my room. "My mom would freak if she knew you were here, in my room . . . alone."

"Yeah, mine too," he says. "You want me to go?"

I smile. "No." It's about making our own choices, not ones our parents have made for us.

He studies the yellow and pink décor of my room, walking around the perimeter. He picks up a pair of red and white boxing gloves I have hanging above my bed. "Yours?"

"I got them when I was in the hospital," I tell him. "You know, to remind me to keep fighting."

He smiles wistfully at the boxing gloves. "I'm tired of fighting. I'm tired of reliving the accident." He says it almost to himself, like it's a private thought he's sharing with me.

I take the gloves from his hand. "Me, too." And for the first time since that fateful night, I mean it. When his eyes bore into mine I ask, "Why are you here? Really."

He shakes his head. "I don't know." He runs his hand over his head, frustrated. "And, God, I know this is crazy and I should stay as far away from you as I can possibly get, but . . . and this part is driving me nuts . . . when I'm close to you I can finally *feel* things again. I laid awake last night thinking about holding you until all the hurt and numbness goes away. Like I need you in order to be sane. I thought it was Kendra, that she'd make me forget. But it's you. *You.* Isn't that fucked up, Maggie? Because maybe if you tell me it's fucked I'll believe it."

"It's not crazy, not by a long shot," I sputter, then go up to him and hug him as tightly as possible.

He puts his arms around me and holds me just as tight. "Could you ever forgive me?" he asks, his voice shaking.

A single tear runs down my cheek. I feel its hot wetness on my skin. I don't know the exact moment it happened, but something has changed. I've changed. And I think it's because I've finally let go of the past. I'm ready to live my life again. "I already have forgiven you, Caleb." I tell him.

We stay that way for a long time. I don't know how much time has passed. It's as if I'm taking away his pain and he's taking away mine. Before, I was confused . . . how I feel about him, how I feel about the accident. But when he's holding me, I let go of the feelings of betrayal I've held onto for the past year. When he pulls back, I hear him sniff, and watch as he wipes his eyes with the back of his hand. "I got something in my eye."

"It's okay to cry, Caleb. I won't tell anybody." I look at my closet, where my racquet is hiding. "I cry a lot."

"Yeah? Well I'm gonna change that."

He's already changed it.

"My mom is going to be home any minute," I say as I stare into mesmerizing clear blue eyes.

"I better go, then."

I nod. "Okay."

He steps closer, so close I can feel his heart beating against mine. I hold my breath when he leans back and puts his palm on my cheek. He lightly brushes my lips with his thumb, tracing my top lip and bottom lip as he moves his thumb across them.

"You have soft lips," he says.

"You already know I'm, uh, not really experienced with kissing," I say shyly, then look down and break our contact. I can't look at him while I say this. "I mean, I'm not really like Kendra in that department. You're probably used to girls who know what they're doing, and I'm new at this and *really, really* embarrassed that I'm doing it badly or wrong or . . . oh, I'm really making a fool out of myself right now."

"I wasn't going to kiss you."

"You weren't?" I look up at him. *Well, of course he wasn't, stupid. Why would he hook up with me when he can be with someone who actually knew what they were doing, someone who isn't responsible for sending him to jail,* my brain tells me.

"Nope. The next time I kiss you I'm gonna take my time, and you said your mom's coming home any minute."

I check the clock on my nightstand and nod.

He bites his bottom lip, deep in thought. "No, the next time I kiss you it'll last a long, long time. And when we're done you're gonna realize being turned on is not about experience."

While I'm still awestruck, Caleb heads out of the house.

THIRTY-ONE
Caleb

It's Sunday. Football Sunday. I'm hanging at Dusty's Sports Bar & Grill with the guys, since we can sit in the dining area and watch the game from the three large screens plastered throughout the restaurant.

The place is run-down—even the dark, wooden tables and chairs wobble because they're so old. But their TV screens are big and new, which brings guys from the closest three towns on Sunday afternoons.

I wonder what Maggie's doing today. She works for Mrs. Reynolds in the mornings, but she'll probably head home early. Is she home now, sitting in her bedroom? Or is she at physical therapy?

"Did you see that, Becker?" Tristan asks as the crowd in the bar groans.

"Sorry, man, I missed it." *I was thinking about someone I have no right thinking about.*

Shaking his head, Tristan points to the screen. "I swear, Guerrera needs some glue on his hands in order to keep the ball in his grip. That's his third fumble."

"Fourth," Drew corrects him.

I'm not into the game today.

I catch Brian looking at the doorway and signaling over whoever just came into the restaurant. I turn around. It's Kendra. Followed by Hannah, Brianne, Danielle, and Sabrina. I don't think their wrestling cheer will go over too well at this place. But then again, maybe it will.

"What are the girls doing here?" a balking Tristan asks Brian, who obviously invited them.

"Can't we change the rules just this once? Kendra really wanted to come."

"Ugh, I'm gonna be sick," Drew says, then fake gags. "She's got you by the balls, man. When are you gonna see it?"

Drew, the self-proclaimed asshole of our group, for the first time in his life is right on. Just as I'm about to proclaim Drew an insightful genius, the girls reach the table. Kendra is wearing tight jeans and a Bears jersey. Brian's jersey, the same one I remember him wearing every Sunday.

Brian is staring at his trophy girl, and it's making me sick too. Because if that's what I looked like when I was dating her, all grateful that a girl like her chose to gift me with being her boyfriend. Someone shoot me right now.

"Can we join you guys?" Kendra asks, but as the words spew out of her mouth she's already pulling up a chair next to Brian and motioning for the girls to find some chairs, too.

Seriously, this is a huge violation of the "no girls allowed for Sunday ball games" code. I can tell Tristan and Drew are not happy about the invasion of chicks. The reason the rule was created in the first place was that we all agreed girls (at least the ones in our group, a.k.a. the ones sitting down at our table right now) are not interested in watching the game. They're interested in breaking our concentration. It's like a challenge, to see if they can distract us from football.

"Hey, Caleb," Danielle says as she parks her chair next to me. "Whatcha been up to?"

Before I can answer, the waitress comes over to our table to slap down our food and ask the girls what they'd like to order.

"What kind of salads do you have?" Brianne asks.

The waitress stifles a laugh. "No salads. We got burgers, chicken sandwiches, wings, and fries. Take your pick."

Brianne is stunned by the choices. I can tell by the way she looks at the waitress in horror. This place is all about the beer/alcohol for the over-twenty-one crowd. Food is the afterthought. "I'll just have a Diet Coke," she finally says.

All of the girls order Diet Cokes. Nothing else. Tristan rolls his eyes.

"Wait!" Sabrina says, calling the waitress back. "I'll have a burger. No cheese, just plain."

"One plain burger, five Diet Cokes," the waitress repeats before retreating.

"I'll have a burger, too," Danielle says, piping in. "Plain, like hers."

"Two burgers, five Diet Cokes."

Brianne raises her eyebrows.

Danielle shrugs. "What? I didn't have lunch and I'm starving. Besides, I'm off the no-carb thing, Brianne."

Drew stands abruptly and puts his hands up. "Okay, if you girls want to join us, there's got to be a few rules. No talking about salads, and I don't even want to hear the word 'carb.' If you didn't come here to talk about the Bears or football, or to reminisce about the year 1985, be silent. And for God's sake, if you don't know which side to root for, I expect no cheering or comments. Got it?"

Kendra's eyebrows are furrowed. "What happened in 1985? Drew, I hate to tell you but we weren't even born yet."

While Drew slaps his forehead in frustration, an embarrassed Brian covers Kendra's mouth. "That was the last year the Bears won the Super Bowl," Brian informs her.

He removes his hand from Kendra's mouth.

"You do know what the Super Bowl is, don't you?" Drew asks, sitting down at last.

"Of course she does," Brian comments, then pulls Kendra close and keeps his arm draped over her shoulders.

The rest of the quarter is met with silence from the

girls and hoots and hollers from the rest of the people in the restaurant. When I happen to glance at Kendra and Brian during a commercial break, her gaze is directed at me as she whispers something in Brian's ear to make him smile mischievously.

I swear I just caught her licking his lobe, too.

Disgusted, I get up and head to the can. After I pee, I wash my hands and lean over the sink while I check out my reflection in the mirror. I'm a fucking mess, unable to just chill and hang out with my friends. Especially not with the girls here. Especially not with Kendra here. She puts my nerves on edge, reminding me of the past. The accident. Maggie.

The door to the men's room opens and sure enough Kendra walks in. I'm not surprised.

"Your boyfriend'll follow you in here," I tell her.

She saunters close to me, close enough I can smell her strong perfume mixed with cherry lip gloss. Total overkill.

"He won't. He thinks you're upset, so I told him I'd talk to you. He trusts us both."

"He's an idiot."

"He also thinks you're jealous. Are you?"

"Oh, yeah," I tell her. She wants to hear it, so I give her what she wants. It's a game she likes to play. I'm tired of playing games, but it's the only way to deal with her.

"You've been elusive, CB."

"Try busy."

"I thought we had an understanding."

The only relationship I want is the one I already have, with Maggie. It might not be public, but it's genuine.

The nagging thing is, I don't know what Kendra knows. Every time we're together, she hints she knows more about the accident than everyone else. But what if she doesn't, what if she's yanking my chain? We were both so plastered that night, and she's a lightweight. Maybe my ex has been playing me this whole time and I'm a sucker just like Brian.

No matter how much I want to, I can't risk alienating her.

She creeps her fiery-red fingertips up my shirt like a spider, stopping when she gets to my shoulder. Then she leans in. "You're like a drug, Caleb. I can't quit."

She's thriving on the chase. Not me. It probably turns her on that someone can walk in any minute and catch us this close together. It's the risk factor giving her the rush. "So why are you suckin' on another guy's ear?" I don't know why I asked. It's not that I even care. I put my hand on her waist, ready to push her away if she comes closer. I'm so done with being her pawn.

"I just wanted to get a reaction out of you. It worked. For the past couple of weeks you've given me nothing, no emotion or encouragement. Brian thinks you're into Maggie Armstrong. Isn't that ridiculous?"

Just when I'm about to answer, the door opens. Drew comes in, seeing Kendra and me standing close, touching each other in what might look like an embrace. It's not what it seems, but it looks bad.

"I'm not even gonna ask," Drew says, then heads to the urinals. Before he slides his zipper down, he turns his head to Kendra. "Do you mind taking this somewhere else?"

"It's nothing I haven't seen before," Kendra says to Drew as she steps away from me, breaking all contact.

Drew gives a short laugh. "Yeah, well you may have made the rounds with my friends, but you ain't getting your hands on mine."

"From what I've heard, one hand would be enough," Kendra shoots back.

"Enough," I say. "Kendra, go back to Brian. Drew, take a leak already."

Hurt that I haven't defended her, she storms out of the men's bathroom, but not before murmuring, "asshole" to Drew on her way out, to which Drew responds, "slut."

Drew finishes, then as he washes his hands he says, "Caleb, you think hooking up with Kendra is the answer? Listen, let Brian have the bitch and move onto someone else."

"It's a little more complicated than that."

Drew makes a tsking noise, just like Mrs. Reynolds. "You're making it complicated."

Then it hits me.

For the second time today, Drew is right on. I'm letting Kendra manipulate me instead of the other way around. I don't need to appease her. I can just let her keep the chase going without giving her a chance to go in for the kill. Wow, I've been going about this whole situation all wrong,

I can't believe the solution is so simple. I take out my wallet and hand Drew a twenty. "Here, pay my bill. I'm outta here."

"You don't have to leave. I'm not gonna tell Brian what you and Kendra were doing."

"At this point, I don't even care," I say, then leave the men's room and head out the back door.

THIRTY-TWO

Maggie

Caleb comes over in the afternoon, totally unexpected. I open the door to answer it and here he is, standing in front of me with a determined look on his face.

"I wanted to see you," is all the explanation I get. "Is your mom home?"

"No. She just left for work five minutes ago."

Caleb and I are friends. Okay, we're more than friends. It's strange and complicated, but it's the only unstrained friendship I have.

I lead him to my room and have him wait there while I bring up some drinks and chips. We sit on the floor and munch on the chips. We talk about school and wrestling, and laugh about the times when we were kids in preschool and the stupid things we did. Then we play gin with the playing cards my mother got me when I was in the hospital. He doesn't talk about kissing at all. He doesn't even look at me with that hot, wanting look I've seen before. He's got something on his mind. I don't know what it is, but it's distracting him.

After a while he puts down the cards and says, "I want to help you, Maggie."

"With what?"

"Playing tennis again. I always see you looking into the closet like there's a monster in there, so I checked it out while you were in the kitchen. I found your racquet."

I stand up. My heart starts racing as I hobble away from him. "I'm never playing again."

He stands, too. "I'm not trying to hurt you, Maggie. I'm trying to help."

I turn my back to him. "I can't play."

"Just try, Maggie. What'll it hurt?"

"I'm not going to be good."

"Who says you have to be good?"

He doesn't know being good at tennis has always meant more than being good at tennis. It's so much deeper than that.

When I look at Caleb, I want to make him proud of me. He's trying to fix whatever pain he's caused me. I want to help him, too. "Okay, I'll try," I say. "But don't expect much."

"I won't."

Fifteen minutes later, we're behind Paradise High looking out across the tennis courts. It brings back memories of me trying to prove myself. Taking a deep breath, I follow Caleb onto the hard, green surface.

When Caleb retrieved my racquet, I froze. I didn't even want to hold it. So after he fetched his own racquet and some tennis balls from his garage, he carried everything without complaint as we walked to the school.

Now he's holding out my racquet to me.

I hesitate.

Taking my hand in his, he wraps my fingers around the racquet handle

"I'm scared," I admit to him.

"Me, too."

I raise an eyebrow.

"Yeah," he says. "If you beat me. I have to keep up my tough-guy image, you know."

That makes me laugh. "You don't need me to make you look tough, Caleb."

With that, he takes the tennis balls and heads to the opposite side of the court. "Be easy on me," he jokes.

He hits the ball right to me, nice and slow. Instincts take over and I hit it back. It feels good, I have to admit, but it also feels strange. My body moves differently now, like I'm stiff and can't loosen up. My legs, my stance, are both awkward and wrong. I can't balance on the balls of my feet and pivot when the ball comes at me. I can't lean over in the ready position, ready to strike at the ball when it flies by.

When Caleb hits the ball back to me, I don't swing.

He stands up and shakes his head. "You could have gotten that."

"I didn't want to. Can we go now?"

"No. Hit this back to me ten times, then we'll go."

He hits the next ball right at me. I hit it lightly.

"Nine," he says, counting down.

Three more balls come within arms length and I gently hit them, so they easily fly over the net right to him. My feet still haven't moved from this spot.

"Six."

Five more gentle balls fly over the net and bounce right in front of me. I send them flying back slowly.

"One more, Maggie. Then we're out of here."

Great. Only one more and the humiliation can end.

He sails one hard and fast over the net. It bounces five feet away from me. I don't even try to get it. He does it again . . . and again. I put my racquet at my side and stare at him. "Are you trying to humiliate me?"

"Stop acting like a baby and go for the ball already," he says, shaking his head. "*Come on.*"

How dare he!

This time, as the ball shoots over the net, my anger and nothing else drives me as I take three steps and whack the ball back at Caleb with all the pent-up power and frustration inside me.

It hits him squarely on his arm. "Ow!" I don't ask him if he's okay, because he has this arrogant look on his face and the corners of his mouth turn up in victory. "Did that feel as good to you as it did to me?" he asks.

I throw the racquet at him and head off the court.

I won't give him the satisfaction of knowing it felt exhilarating and awesome.

He steps beside me and pulls me to him. "I'm gonna have a bruise, you know," he says. "But watching you whack that thing was damn hot."

I look over at the welt growing on his arm. "It was?"

In a swift motion, he moves forward and pins me against the fence with his body. "I'm going to kiss you."

My stomach does a little flip; I forget about being mad. My nerves take over all emotions. "Here?"

"Oh, yeah. Right here, right now. You gonna run away this time?"

"I don't think so, but I'm not sure."

He smiles, amused at my answer.

I look up into his eyes that give me a glimpse into his private world, then lick my lips in anticipation.

And that is the beginning of our kissing marathon. All I have to say is that I don't feel inexperienced after an hour of lips and tongues and innocent and not-so-innocent caresses on both sides. I don't feel insecure about kissing anymore.

We moved from the courts to the park and back to my bedroom. On my bed. Caleb leans back and moans. "We have to stop this or my body is going to suffer aftershocks for days."

Relaxing, I lay my head on his chest. "That was nice."

"Yeah, too nice."

He's breathing heavily. We both are. I take a deep, slow breath and bask in the moment. I could stay here forever, just like this. Gazing. Feeling wanted. Feeling protected. Feeling normal.

"I should hate you for making me play tennis."

"Yeah. But you can't, can you? Besides, we've had a makeout session you'll be thinking about for weeks."

"You've got an ego problem."

"Only with you." He chuckles, then yawns.

"Do I bore you?" I ask.

"Not at all," he says, stroking my hair. "It's just . . . I don't sleep too well. And I'm so relaxed and content my body is ready to crash."

I lean up on my elbows. "So sleep."

"Here?"

"Sure. My mom won't be home until late." I start to get up, to leave him my whole bed so he could sleep in peace.

"Don't leave me," he says. "Lie next to me." He pulls me down with him. "You're so different," he says almost to himself.

"Don't say that," I tell him, looking away. I want to keep the false fantasy that I'm the same as other girls, at least for a little while.

"Different in a good way." His brows furrow. "A really good way."

Then he pulls me tight against him. We're spooned together as if we've been dating for years. We're even sharing the pillow I've slept on since I was ten. The last thing I remember before waking up is Caleb's slow, rhythmic breathing behind me as he falls into slumber.

But now I hear the front door open and I'm fully awake. "Caleb, wake up. My mom's home."

It takes him a second to get his bearings, we've been sleeping for over five hours.

"Wait here and don't make a sound," I say, then kiss him on his sleepy lips.

Sliding out from beneath his arm pinning me to him, I close my bedroom door and head downstairs. "Hey, Mom," I say, my voice groggy from sleep.

"I didn't mean to wake you, sweetheart. I hate these late Sunday nights, but I'd rather have them and be able to spend the mornings with you. It seems we spend much too little time together lately." She puts down her purse and starts climbing the stairs. I pray she doesn't want to hang out in my room and have one of those mother/daughter talks. Not now. But I guess if she does, the truth will come out. Maybe it would be a blessing in disguise, but I'd rather not chance it.

"It's fine, Mom. You always worry about the small stuff."

She doesn't hear the creak of my bed behind my door. But I do.

Mom's eyebrows furrow. "Why are you sleeping in your clothes?"

Oops. "I was in my room and must have dozed."

"Well, I'm beat, too. Go back to bed. You have school in the morning. And change out of those clothes."

"Okay. Good night." I hope she doesn't realize I'm anticipating with bated breath the moment she closes the door to her room.

When she closes her bedroom door, I hurry back to my room. Caleb is sitting on my bed, startled. "I'm so sorry," he whispers, still looking as dangerous and cool as ever even half-asleep. "I lost track of time."

"Me, too."

He walks over to the window.

"Caleb, what are you doing?" I whisper.

"Finding a way out."

I put my hand on his arm and tug on it. "You're not jumping out my window. Just wait fifteen minutes and I'll lead you to the front door. My mom sleeps like the dead and she falls asleep really fast. Besides, if we get caught we're in this together. Right?"

It takes him a while to respond. It's almost as if he doesn't believe what I just said. "Yeah. Right," he finally murmurs.

THIRTY-THREE

Caleb

I met with Damon this morning, after convincing my parents I stayed out late because I was at Brian's and we lost track of time. They bought it. Damon came for some sort of evaluation for the State of Illinois. He interviewed my family, even Leah, then we hung out in my room while he grilled me with questions.

I told Damon I asked Maggie to see her leg, leaving out the part that we work together every weekday after school, or the fact that she's the only person who makes me forget the past year even happened. God forbid I should tell him I slept with her last night, in the literal sense of the word.

Damon shakes his head. "It's forbidden to confront your victim, Caleb."

"I didn't confront her."

Damon crosses my room and puts his hand to his head as if he has a headache. "You sweet on her?"

"Who?"

"Maggie."

"No. No way," I lie.

"You small town kids are a breed apart. Okay, here's the deal: stay away from her."

"Do I have a choice?"

"No." Damon opens his folder and clicks his pen. "You're almost done with your community-service requirements. A gazebo for Mrs. Dorothy Reynolds. I see you've been on that job for three weeks."

"If all goes well I should be done by the end of next week."

Damon seems impressed. "Good work, Caleb. You started out rocky, but you're a decent kid. Let's meet again next week and talk about what's going to happen after your release."

I'm feeling energized after Damon's visit, knowing the jail threat is almost behind me. I just have to keep the fact that I'm with Maggie a secret.

I knock on my sister's door. She's in there. Her room is her cave. My sister hibernates except for school and meals.

She doesn't answer, so I knock louder. "Leah, open up."

"What do you want?" she says through the door.

I sigh. This is harder than I thought. "Just open the fucking door."

She opens it a crack. I push it the rest of the way open and walk inside. It's too dark in here so I pull the shade up.

"Keep it down."

"Yeah, well, we have to talk and I can't see a damn thing."

"I don't want to talk."

"Too bad," I say, my hands crossed in front of my chest.

Leah's gripping the handle of the door, like she's ready to flee.

"Are Mom and Dad home?" she asks nervously.

"They're out."

She lets out a small breath.

I don't even know where to start. I just know I'm ready to say it out loud. It's been pent up inside of me for over a year. The demon's got to get loose. Life is not about covering up for crap and living in a fantasy world.

I take a deep breath and tell my sister, "You hit Maggie with the car and I took the fall for it. It sucked, but it's over. I wouldn't have done it if I knew you'd act like a fucking corpse the rest of your life."

Her eyes are wide as if her brain is registering the truth for the first time.

"Talk, Leah," I order. "Say something . . . *anything!*"

"I can't deal with it!" she cries out, then hurls herself onto her bed face-first.

I grab a box of tissues off her nightstand and toss it to her. I stand over her as she cries hysterically.

"I'm sorry, Caleb. I'm *so* sorry," she says between sobs. "I could have killed her, Caleb."

"But you didn't."

"I stood there and watched as they handcuffed you. I let them take you away."

I was so used to being the troublemaker, used to being the one who screwed up. Leah had been the squeaky-clean twin; I was the rebel. Even drunk, I didn't hesitate taking the fall for the accident. Leah wasn't going to be handcuffed, arrested, and convicted. She couldn't handle it. I could.

The cops didn't question it when I confessed right there. Hell, my own parents never questioned my guilt.

To think, it was all because Leah swerved to avoid hitting a fucking squirrel in the road.

"It's over." I tell her.

"No, Caleb, it's not. It'll never be over. I'm going to carry this guilt around with me the rest of my life. I can't even look at Maggie. Hell, Caleb, I can't even look at you. It's so hard for me, you can't imagine what it's like."

She's right, I can't.

Turning to me, she sucks in a frightened breath. "You're not going to tell anyone, are you? Promise me you'll never tell *anyone*."

I look down at my twin, the girl who I shared my

mom's womb with, shared birthdays with, and grew up side by side with. She should know me like I know her, feel my pain as much as I feel hers. She knows this secret is tearing me up inside. I can feel it just as much as I know how twisted her rationale has become. But she ignores me and focuses only on herself. She really is, after all, a stranger to me.

THIRTY—FOUR

Maggie

I'm humming an old song my mom used to sing to me when she put me to bed, back when I was scared of the dark and refused to go to sleep. Life was less complicated back then. My dad lived at home and Mom's only job was, well, to just be a mom.

Now she's working as a waitress and dating. Okay, that last part is my fault. I can't even blame my mom for her date tonight. Thanks to Caleb, I'm finally coming to terms with it.

That first night he kissed me was magical. I was all ready to just be friends with him, cherish our platonic relationship, when it suddenly turned into something more. When I'm with him I don't think about my limp. All I think about is how good it feels to be able to talk and share and kiss.

Am I falling in love with Caleb Becker again? I don't know. I'm so nervous and scared to be hurt again, I'm keeping a wall up so my heart is protected.

Little by little he's been chipping away at that wall.

After work we've been getting off the bus two blocks away so we could steal an extra few minutes together. Unfortunately, today he had a meeting with some counselor from the Department of Corrections. He said it was important, so I hope it goes well.

I've forgiven him for the accident. Two days ago he tried to bring it up, saying he had something important to tell me about it. I cut him off with a kiss and promises of forgiveness.

The wind is blowing, and the leaves are starting to fall. It's the end of summer. The trees and grass and flowers are getting ready for dormancy. As I plant the last of the daffodil bulbs for Mrs. Reynolds, I think of the winter they'll have to survive before thawing and being ready for their first peek of the sun.

I look up from daydreaming about songs and trees and Caleb to find Mrs. Reynolds standing over me. I stop humming.

"You sure are cheery today."

"I only have five more bulbs before I'm all done," I tell her.

"That's a good thing, too," she says, looking up at the

darkening sky. "The weather is changing. I already feel a winter chill in the air."

"Me too." After I finish the last bulb, we sit down and eat dinner.

"I'd like to invite you and your mother over for dinner one night. But only if it's okay with you."

"Why wouldn't it be?"

"Because my son has been on more dates with your mother than he's been on in the past three years. I've been coaching him, you know."

"You have?"

"Did Lou bring you chocolates the first time he came to your house?"

I nod.

"That was my advice. I told him to bring yellow roses to your mom because they're the best way to start—"

"They weren't yellow roses."

She raises an eyebrow. "They weren't?"

"No. Tulips."

"Yellow?"

"Purple."

"Hmm. And the chocolates, they were caramels?"

"Frango mints. Very tasty."

"Tasty, huh? So much for mother's advice."

I laugh.

My boss waves her arms in the air. "Enough lollygagging, Margaret."

When we're putting the dishes away, Mrs. Reynolds sways and holds the edge of the counter for support.

"Are you okay?" I ask, taking the plate from her and leading her to the sofa.

"These new medications are just wreaking havoc with these old bones, that's all. Nothing to worry about."

I do worry. Before I leave her house, I call Auntie Mae's Diner and tell Mr. Reynolds to check on her.

I head to the bus stop after I'm convinced she's okay. A car screeches by me as I walk. I recognize it as the same car with the guys who got in a fight with Caleb.

"Hey, it's Caleb Becker's retarded girlfriend," someone yells out the window.

I bite the inside of my lip and keep walking.

"I think she wants you, Vic. Why don't you show her a good time," someone else says. Then they all laugh.

The car is driving slowly beside me. I just hope they don't step out of the car. If I stop walking, will they get out?

Will they hurt me?

Deep fear, so intense I'm shaking inside, keeps me from stopping.

I can't go back to Mrs. Reynolds' house. It's too far and I can't outrun these guys. There are houses lining the street. I could try ringing a doorbell and ask someone to call the police.

A plan forms in my head. I turn around and head in the opposite direction, the direction I just came from. But in the process I fall down. My hands are stinging and I feel sticky wetness dripping down my knee from the cut I've just gotten from the fall.

"Did you have a nice trip?" one of them yells out the window.

I get up and hobble faster, praying they won't turn the car around and follow me. Because if they do, I don't know how I'm going to handle it. I listen for the sound of the car turning around. I don't dare look back and give them another reason to come after me. But I can hardly hear anything besides the furious panting of my own breath.

Relief sweeps over me as the bus roars down the street. I hurry to the curb and wave the bus down, then glance to see if the car is still there.

"You okay?" the bus driver asks.

"I'm fine," I say, then scurry to the back to sit.

Nothing can cure me, no amount of physical therapy or surgeries. The old Maggie, the tennis star without a debilitating limp, the old Maggie, who could run away from danger, doesn't even exist.

Caleb is outside mowing his lawn as I limp down the street. He stops the motor and rushes over to me as soon as he glances my way.

"What happened? Tell me what happened."

I'm trying to hold back tears. "I'm fine."

He looks around to make sure people aren't looking, then cradles my face in his hands. "You're not fine. Damn it, talk to me."

I gaze at him in despair. "It was that Vic guy."

"I'll kill him if he touched you," he growls, eyeing my ripped pants stained with blood.

"He didn't. He and his friends just scared me, that's all."

"I'll make sure that never happens again, Maggie."

I smile warmly at him. "You're not going to always be able to protect me. What are you going to do when I'm in Spain, fly over and beat up all the bad guys who make fun of me?"

THIRTY-FIVE
Caleb

I said Vic was going to pay, but I didn't know how to do it . . . legally. That is, until I was talking to the guys at lunch yesterday who told me Vic is competing for his school at our wrestling invitational today.

I am officially a Paradise Panther wrestler now. And I only have to beat out four guys until I come face to face on the mat with Medonia. As I suspected, we're still in the same weight class. I think the guy's using steroids to bulk up.

I'm in the locker room with the rest of the team, getting ready for the match.

"Caleb, you look like you're about to kill someone," Brian says as I jump rope to warm up.

"He's in *the zone*," Drew says. "Ain't that right?"

I don't answer. Coach Wenner stops me and pats me on the back. "You haven't been to practice, Becker. You sure you're ready?"

I put my mouth guard in. "Yeah, Coach."

I win my first two matches with a pin within the first minute. The third match took me a little longer. I think I pinned him in ninety seconds.

"CB's on fire!" Tristan yells as he's plugging up a nose-bleed from his previous match.

I focus as they call me and Medonia up to the mat. I can't wait to wipe that smirk off his face.

"How's your girlfriend?" he asks.

"Better than yours, any day."

"She's a cripple, Becker."

"You'll be the cripple after this match."

The ref puts his hands between us. "Keep it clean, guys."

When the match starts, I push him with all my might until he falls. Unfortunately, he rolls off the mat and the ref blows his whistle. "Caution, Panthers. Point for Fremont."

The next time we start, Medonia starts low. I move off the mat when the match starts and Medonia flies past me.

The ref blows his whistle.

When the match starts up again, I get one more caution for an illegal hold which ends up with my elbow in Medonia's face.

One more caution and I'll be disqualified.

The whistle blows, and the ref calls out, "We've got a bleeder for Fremont. Two minute break."

Coach Wenner stalks over to me, eyes blazing. "What are you doing? My team doesn't play dirty, Becker. Now either you go out there and try to win that match, or I'm forfeiting it for you. Which is it?"

THIRTY-SIX

Maggie

Mrs. Reynolds is going to be the death of me. She's determined to make me get behind the wheel of her black monstrosity sitting in the garage.

"It's a classic," Mrs. Reynolds says, her chin held high as the garage door opens and reveals the Cadillac.

"I'm . . . I'm really not ready to drive yet," I say. "But you can drive it and I'll ride on the passenger side."

Mrs. Reynolds opens the passenger door and slides into the seat. "Honey, my eyes can hardly see two feet in front of me. Come on, now. Time's a-wastin'."

She hangs her hand out the window, the keys dangling from her fingers. She shakes them, the keys on the ring clinking against each other.

I'm huffing and puffing as I slip the keys from her hand, hoping she'll get the hint. She doesn't. I open the driver's

side door and slide into the front seat. Wow. The white leather is soft, and the back of the seat is as big as an old Lay-Z-Boy recliner. I look out the front window. The hood is wide and has that shiny Cadillac symbol.

I turn to Mrs. Reynolds, who has her small purse neatly clutched in her lap, ready to go. Making the old lady proud of me would be so great. But . . . I'm not ready. I think.

"I can't do this," I explain, hoping she'll understand.

She's having none of it. Just by the stern look on her face, I know. "Margaret, put the key in the ignition."

I do it.

"Now turn the key and start the car."

I turn the key.

"What are you afraid of, dear?"

"Hitting someone. Getting into an accident." I gulp.

"This part of you has to change, you know. Being afraid to take chances is scarier than actually doing things that challenge you."

"I haven't driven since the accident."

"It's about time you did, then."

I shake my head.

"Back up slowly so you don't hit the fence." Mrs. Reynolds faces forward and buckles her seat belt.

I buckle mine, too. I have no clue why the lady can

make me do things I don't want to do. It's like she has this power over me.

I take a deep breath, press my foot on the brake, and put the car into reverse. Slowly releasing the brake, I turn back and make sure I'm all clear to back out of the driveway.

"Watch out for the mailbox," Mrs. Reynolds advises.

We're safe at the bottom of the driveway and I back out into the street. I'm trying to convince myself not to have a panic attack, but I don't think I'm being too successful. Part of me is excited to drive again and get that fear out of my life, but the other, stronger part of me, wants to put the car in park and limp home. I hear Caleb's voice inside my head, pushing me to do it.

Mrs. Reynolds pats me on the knee. "Well done, Margaret."

With that vote of confidence, I put the car into drive and slowly head down the street.

My feet aren't used to the pedals and I'm stopping too hard and accelerating too fast. "Sorry," I say after we come to a stop sign and Mrs. Reynolds jerks forward.

She clears her throat. "No problem. Let's take it a little easy on the accelerator and brake, shall we?"

"Uh, sure." But when it's my turn to cross the intersection, I take my foot off the brake and gently put pressure on the accelerator. I pump it a bit because I don't want to jerk Mrs. Reynolds forward again.

But now I'm making it worse. Oops. "You'd probably

be a better driver, even with your vision problems," I say seriously.

"I might have to agree with you, dear. Next time we try this, remind me to take some Dramamine."

I give her a sideways glance. "You look like you're going to be sick."

"Just look at the road, not at me," she orders. "My looking sick has nothing to do with your driving."

She directs me to a place called Monique's. It has cute dresses in the window. By the time we get there my nerves have gone from overdrive to idle. I follow Mrs. Reynolds into the store. Dresses in all colors and patterns are positioned on racks throughout the store.

Mrs. Reynolds runs her fingers over a short, light blue silk dress. "Do you know how to spot quality material?"

I take my hand and run the soft cloth through my fingers. "I've never really paid attention to fabrics."

"Every fabric has its own personality, just like my daffodils. For some, the softness and weight matters. For others, it's the way the fabric moves . . . and you can't discount color vibrancy."

"How do you know so much?"

"Honey, when you're as old as I am, you know more than you want to know."

A woman who works at the store comes up to us, wearing a plum pant suit and blonde hair that's neatly combed and curled at the ends. "Can I help you ladies?"

"We're looking for a dress," Mrs. Reynolds says, then points to me. "For this young lady."

"For me?" I say, following behind as the lady leads us through the store.

Mrs. Reynolds stops and turns to me. "You need a little something to spice up your wardrobe, Margaret. All you wear are solids and, to be completely honest, your clothes are a bit too big and casual."

I look down at my black cotton pants and grey t-shirt. "They're comfortable."

"And totally appropriate for lounging around the house. But, we're having dinner tonight and I want you to dress up. Consider it an early Christmas gift."

The saleswoman leads us to a rack of short cocktail dresses. "These just came in from Europe. It's a new silk/washable blend."

Mrs. Reynolds slides the silky, teal-colored dress between her fingers. "Too stiff. She's used to cotton, so I'd like a softer fabric."

"I don't wear short dresses," I tell them.

The lady leads us to another corner of the store. "How about a cotton/wool blend?"

Mrs. Reynolds shakes her head. "Too hot."

"Rayon?"

"Too clingy."

I'd expect the lady to get frustrated, but she just puts her hand to her chin in thought. "I may have something that you'd like in the back. Wait here." She goes to the back of the store and comes out a minute later with a yellow dress hanging off her arm. Holding it out to Mrs. Reynolds, she says, "It's from Sweden. A new supplier sent it to us for evaluation."

Mrs. Reynolds eyes the dress, then rubs the edge of the fabric between her thumb and forefinger. "Love the fabric, but the color is atrocious. She'd look like a sour lemon in this."

"It came in a light plum color, too. I'll go get it."

"It's a beautiful shade," I say when she brings out the plum-colored dress. I try it on in the dressing room. It has spaghetti straps and a scooped neckline. The middle is cinched at the waist before waves of the material flow down and stop just above my ankle. When I walk in front of the mirror you can hardly tell I have a limp.

The sales woman smiles when I model it for them. "I think we have a winner here."

Mrs. Reynolds smacks her lips together. "It's perfect. We'll take it."

"You have a very generous grandmother," the saleswoman says to me.

I look over at Mrs. Reynolds, who is across the store looking at another dress. "I know. I couldn't have picked a better one myself."

When I go back to the dressing room to take the dress off, Mrs. Reynolds stops me. "Keep it on, Margaret. We'll be going to dinner from here and you won't have time to change."

"Which dress are you trying on?"

"Old ladies don't need new dresses. Now stop the chatter and let's move on."

I put my hands on my cinched, plum-covered hips. "I'm not leaving this store until you buy a new dress, too."

Mrs. Reynolds' mouth opens in shock.

"Don't look so startled, *Grandma*," I say, copying her famous saying to me. "It doesn't suit your face."

Her mouth snaps shut. Then she throws her head back and howls with unabashed laughter.

A half hour later we're back in the Cadillac. I might also add that Mrs. Reynolds is wearing a new silk and rayon, powder-blue dress with a matching jacket.

"I want you to deduct money out of my paycheck for the dress. I insist," I say.

Mrs. Reynolds just smiles without responding.

"I'm serious, Mrs. Reynolds."

"I know you are, dear, and I appreciate it. But I'm still buying it with my own funds."

I shake my head in frustration. "Where to now?"

"A pie run."

"Huh?"

"Just head for Auntie Mae's Diner and you'll see."

I steer the car around and drive to the diner.

Mrs. Reynolds ducks down. "Go to the back, where the dumpster is," she whispers. "And don't let anyone see you."

The woman is serious. I slide down in the seat and creep the car toward the back of the restaurant as if we're here to rob the place. I stop near the dumpsters. "What are we doing here?" I whisper, then wonder why I'm whispering. Her son owns the restaurant.

"Keep the car running, just get out and knock on the back door three times. Then you pause for two seconds and then knock another three times." Mrs. Reynolds sinks lower into her seat. "When someone answers, say, *The red hen has flown the coop.*"

"I don't get it."

"You will if you follow my directions. Now go!"

This is comical. I almost pee in my dress as I creep up to the back door and knock. Knock, knock, knock. Pause. Knock, knock, knock.

Juan, one of the bus boys, opens the door a crack.

I burst out laughing as I say, "The red bird has flown the coop."

"Don't you mean *hen*?"

"Oh, yeah. Sorry, sorry, sorry. I mean *The red hen has flown the coop.*"

I think Juan is laughing as he says, "Wait here," and closes the door. When the door opens, Irina hands me two boxes.

"What's inside?" I say.

"Don't ask me, Moggie. A surprise for you and Mrs. Reynolds."

When she closes the door, I bring the boxes to the car and slide into the driver's seat. "We got the goods."

"Great, now head back to my house."

Mrs. Reynolds is smirking as I drive up to her house. When I pull up to the garage, I finally figure out what this is all about.

The gazebo is finished, and Caleb has hung white lights all around it. White candles are lit inside, making the whole gazebo light up. Caleb is standing beside it, wearing khaki pants and a white dress shirt and tie.

When he winks at me and flashes his smile, I feel another piece of armor chipping away.

THIRTY-SEVEN

Caleb

I hurry to the car and open the door for Mrs. Reynolds. I hold out my hand and help her out of the car. "You look hot," I tell her.

She pats me on the cheek and says, "If I was only sixty years younger, sonny boy."

"Did you do what I said?" I say close to her ear.

She snorts. "I had Margaret saying that ridiculous sentence we came up with."

Mrs. Reynolds and I are partners in crime tonight. The gazebo is finished. My job here is done. I had the old lady make Maggie drive around town until six o'clock. I've been putting this night together in my head for a week already. A perfect night.

When I turn and catch sight of Maggie, I'm doomed. And speechless.

Mrs. Reynolds says, "Don't look so startled, Caleb. It doesn't suit your face."

Maggie walks up to me, the dress showing off curves I only recently dreamed she had.

"The gazebo looks great," she says.

I don't look away from her. Hell, I can't take my eyes off of her. These two unlikely women are my saving grace.

Maggie blushes, then glides away to join Mrs. Reynolds in the gazebo.

I've set a table inside the gazebo, complete with a three-course meal, compliments of my saved-up lawn mowing allowance and Little Italy Restaurant. I added a little spot heater to keep the gazebo warm, and have a portable radio with music playing softly in the background.

After pulling out a chair for Maggie, I hold my hand out to Mrs. Reynolds. "Would you care to dance, milady?"

She laughs, but I take her hand and pull her into a spin and into my arms. She shrieks. "Caleb, please. I'm an old lady. Where's my cane?"

"I thought old ladies like younger men," I tease, and dance slowly until the song is over.

I lead her to her chair and pull it out. "You better watch out for him, Margaret. He's dangerous."

I wince as I bend down to sit.

"What's wrong?" Maggie asks.

"Nothing," I say after everyone has been served. I take a spoonful of the minestrone and look up. Maggie's not buying it. Neither is Mrs. Reynolds. "Okay, okay. I competed in a wrestling invitational today. No big deal."

"I didn't know you joined the team."

"It was a one-time thing. I think."

Mrs. Reynolds finishes her soup and waves the spoon at me. "You might have a broken rib."

"I'm sure it's just bruised," I say, trying to reassure her as much as myself. Right before I pinned Vic in the second round, he knocked me to the ground and took a five-pointer.

I won the match, but the coach still gave me hell for playing dirty the first round.

"I can't wait until the daffodils bloom," Maggie says, her eyes sparkling with the candles shining on them. My hands are clammy from nervousness, I have no clue why. "You're going to have to take a picture for me and send it to Spain."

I still can't believe she's leaving. Just when I fell for her.

"Speaking of Spain . . ." Mrs. Reynolds hands her an envelope. "Enjoy your journey, but always remember where you came from."

Maggie raises a glass with water filled in it. "Who can forget Paradise?"

We clink our glasses together.

After we eat, I open the boxes from Irina, the chef from Auntie Mae's. As I set samples of pies in front of

Maggie and Mrs. Armstrong, you'd swear they were related by the elated expressions on their faces.

We all take a fork and dig in.

"This has been the most magnificent day of my life since Albert died, may he rest in peace. Thank you both. But these weary bones need a rest."

"Are you okay?" Maggie asks, concern lacing her voice. We both get up to help her.

"No, you two sit down and enjoy. I just need to rest a bit."

Regardless to what the old lady is claiming, Maggie helps her upstairs while I clear the dishes. "She okay?" I ask when Maggie comes back outside.

"I think so. She went to the doctor yesterday. He wants to run some tests on her, but she's too stubborn to go."

I watch Maggie. God, anyone who's with her is infected by her humility and honesty. "Care to dance?"

"I can't," she says. "Not with my leg . . ."

I take her hand in mine and lead her back into the gazebo. "Dance with me, Maggie," I urge as I put one arm around her back and pull her close.

We sway to the music. Slowly she relaxes into my arms. "I never imagined it would be like this," she says into my chest.

When her leg starts to hurt, I clear a place on the floor and we lie side by side next to each other.

"What did you ever see in Kendra?" she asks.

Hell, I don't know. "She was popular and pretty. Someone

who all the guys wished they could date. She used to look at me as if I was the only guy who could ever make her happy'

She sits up. "Okay, now you sound like a jerk."

"I was one."

She lies next to me, my arm as her pillow.

We watch the candles burn down one by one. When there's only one candle left, I kiss her soft lips and trace her curves with my hands until she's breathless and weak.

"Let me see your scars," I say when we're both panting and coming up for air from making out. I take the hem of her dress in my fist and slowly slide the material up.

She stills my hand with her own and smoothes the material back down. "No."

"Trust me."

"I . . . I can't," she murmurs. "Not with my scars."

Her words hit me like a cell door slamming closed. Because even if she thinks she forgave me, even if she made promises of forgiveness, even if she kisses me like I'm her hero, I finally realize she can't get over her anger inside. And never will fully trust me.

I lie back, totally frustrated, and lay my arm over my eyes. "This isn't going to work, is it?"

Maggie sits up. "I'm trying," she says, her voice full of regret.

I want to tell Maggie I wasn't responsible for hurting her leg, but I can't. What if Leah was right? I can't let my sister go to jail when I've already paid for her mistake. I'm committed to living with that blame forever.

The night of the accident, I was supposed to drive Leah home. But I was too drunk and enraged from Maggie's accusations. Staying with Kendra and making sure she didn't go home with any other guy was more important than anything else. My fucking ego. I had no idea Leah took my keys until she came back to the party ranting like a lunatic about an accident.

The rest, as they say, is history.

THIRTY-EIGHT

Maggie

◆

I had everything I wanted and I screwed it up. Caleb loved me, all I had to do was show him my scars to prove to him how much I trust and love him back.

But I couldn't. Something was pulling me back into my protective shell.

I told my mom I was too sick to go to school today, so I'm lying in bed. The dress Mrs. Reynolds bought me is hanging in my closet, a cruel reminder of the most romantic evening of my life. I won Caleb and lost him just as quick.

When he took me home and we parted, he gave me a small smile and said we've always been friends, and we'd remain friends.

That's the most important thing. Right?

So why have I been crying the entire morning?

I call Mrs. Reynolds' house to see how she's doing after last night.

Mr. Reynolds answers the phone. "Hello?" he says, his voice shaken.

"Hi, it's Maggie . . . Margaret. Is Mrs. Reynolds there?"

Mr. Reynolds doesn't say anything for a long time, and my throat gets a huge lump in it.

"My mom died this morning, Maggie."

"No," I whisper as my life comes crashing down on me. "It can't be true. We were together. Last night she was dancing and laughing and—"

"She was grateful to have you in her life," he says. "She loved you as a granddaughter. More than that, she loved you as a friend."

"Where is she? Was she alone when she died?"

Mr. Reynolds sniffles. "They just took her away in an ambulance. She died in her sleep, no pain. Her heart has been bad for years, Maggie. It was only a matter of time."

Tears roll down my cheeks as I remember the times we spent in the past few months. She taught me so much about life. "The daffodils . . . she'll never see the daffodils come up," I say, stifling my emotions.

"Mama loved those daffodils, didn't she?"

I don't know what else to say to him. Mrs. Reynolds may have been up in years, but there was so much she still had planned. Having my mom and me over for dinner, watching the daffodils bloom in the spring. Eating Irina's pies.

"I'll miss her."

"I know you will. She never wanted a funeral. She said they're just an excuse for depressed people to make senseless chatter."

I smile wistfully. "That sounds like her." She just accused me of it yesterday, which reminds me . . . "A dress. She bought a dress."

"The blue one slung over the chair in her bedroom?"

"Yeah. If she's going to be buried . . ." I can't even get out the words.

"I'll make sure of it. Listen, if you want to come over and take something from the house before we sell it, you can."

"You can't sell the house." The daffodils, the gazebo . . . everything she cared about in the last two months are for nothing.

In the evening, my mom drives me over to Mrs. Reynolds house for the last time. She's holding my hand as Lou greets us. "Take anything you want, Maggie."

In the laundry room, all clean and folded, is the muumuu.

I pick it up and clutch it to my chest. It was Mrs. Reynolds' way of protecting me, covering my clothes so I wouldn't get dirty. "Can I have this?" I ask.

Mr. Reynolds seems surprised I'd want it, but says, "I was serious when I said *anything*."

There's two more things I want. I head to the kitchen and open cabinets until I find it. My mom is shrugging to Mr. Reynolds, who is as baffled as her. "It's got to be around here somewhere. Aha." I open one of the top drawers and on a piece of old, stained and ripped linen paper is her favorite Snickerdoodle cookie recipe.

"Anything else?"

"One more thing."

Mom and Mr. Reynolds follow me up to the attic. I head for the trunk and open it up. Holding up a picture frame, I say "This is the last thing."

Mr. Reynolds says, "It's yours."

I stare at the picture of two people madly in love on their wedding day.

May they both rest in peace.

THIRTY—NINE

Caleb

Maggie wasn't at school yesterday, and I haven't seen her all morning. Twice today I've passed by her locker, but she's been as elusive as a ghost.

During third period I can't focus. So I take the bathroom pass and head out the door. But I don't head straight to the bathroom. I turn the corner and go down the hall where I know her locker is. I've turned into a stalker.

"Looking for someone, Caleb?" It's Kendra, with a hall pass of her own dangling from her fingers. "Maggie Armstrong, perhaps?"

"Stop playing games with me, Kend."

She flashes a wicked smile. "No, seriously. I just don't get what you see in her."

"Nothing," I say just to get my ex off my back. "I see nothing in Maggie Armstrong. If anything she's been a distraction because I can't have you." The bullshit is flying because I need to protect Maggie and Leah at all costs.

The sound of someone behind me makes me turn around. It's Maggie. She's heard every lying word out of my mouth.

Kendra slinks toward her. "Caleb, did you tell Maggie the truth about the accident?"

"Kendra. Don't," I say in a warning tone. "Or I'll clue Brian in about what's been going on between you and me. Isn't your dad's election next week?"

If Kendra had claws, they'd be out and she'd be murderous.

Maggie hobbles toward me. "What's been going on between you and Kendra, Caleb?"

Kendra puts her hands on her hips, ready for this battle to begin. "Yeah, Caleb. Tell her how many times we've been together since you came back."

What can I say? I want to tell Maggie the truth, I'm going to tell her the truth. About everything. But not here, not in front of Kendra. She's got nothing to do with me and Maggie.

"Say something," Maggie orders, her eyes on fire.

When I don't, she slaps me and limps away.

———

I hate pep rallies. So I find it insane that I'm stuck in the middle of one today, of all days. But here I am, in the center of the crowd of athletes while the cheerleaders lead the rest of the school in pepping the entire student body.

As if a bunch of wrestlers want to be "peppy." But the guys'll take any excuse to ditch class for an hour.

Meyer stands at the podium as if he's the president of the United States instead of principal of a small-town school. "Settle down, everyone. Settle down." The place is still noisy, but it's the best he's going to get and he knows it. "This is a time to celebrate the students who represent the Paradise Panthers in athletics."

The crowd starts getting restless, the gymnasium floor vibrating from the noise.

"Settle down. Settle down. We're going to honor our athletes this afternoon. Each coach is going to come up and announce the members of their teams. Let's start with our largest team . . . football!"

This sets the cheerleaders into a frenzy, kicking and cartwheeling all over the gym.

"Put your hand up when I call your name," the football coach says. "Adam Albers, Nate Atkins, Max Ballinski, Ty Edmonds . . ." The list goes on and on for what seems like forever.

I'm standing next to Brian. "This is torture, man."

"Tell me about it," he says.

But when Coach Wenner gets up to the podium, the guys on the Paradise wrestling team are never ones to take a back seat. A roar goes up behind me. "Wee-ner! Wee-ner! Wee-ner!"

The guys are pronouncing the coach's name wrong on purpose. I bet Wenner is already planning how many extra push-ups he'll make the team do in practice to make up for it.

The rest of the school gets into it, even as the teachers are trying to put a kabash on the latest chant.

"Wee-ner! Wee-ner."

"Okay, ha ha, very funny. You had your laugh, now let's get to it," Coach says. "Andy Abrams, Caleb Becker, Adrian Cho, David Grant . . ."

Even though our school is small, it takes a while to get through all the names.

Finally, after more than an hour stuck in this hot gym, Meyer gets back on the mic and dismisses us to our sixth period classes. Trying to get out is like a mob scene. Everyone is as restless as I am to escape. But I'm hanging back.

I scan the bleachers. My sister is looking down, oblivious to anything except the stairs. Maggie is standing with the rest of the mob pushing through to get out. She looks so fragile standing there, like a bird surrounded by an elephant stampede.

There's some pushing and shoving. Two junior guys are fighting. And it's right where Maggie is. "Maggie, watch out!" I yell, but she can't hear me. She doesn't notice the commotion behind her, but I'm too late and it's too noisy. The guy is pushed into Maggie, who trips over two steps and lands flat on her knee.

"Maggie!" I yell, pushing people out of the way to get

to her. I finally reach her and kneel next to her. "Maggie, you okay?"

She blinks, looks like she's going to be sick, and sits up.

"Mag-ie, Mag-ie, Mag-ie," the crowd starts chanting.

I look up at the crowd and yell, "Shut the fuck up!" but nobody is listening. I grab Maggie's elbow. She tries to pull away but I hang on tight. "Are you okay?" I ask once she's standing. Most of the kids have stopped chanting her name, but a few assholes still have nothing better to do.

Drew grabs my shoulder and pulls me back. "Caleb, what are you helping her for? The bitch was responsible for putting you in jail."

I take my fist and slam it right into Drew's face. He charges me and we're at each other's throats, fists flying, until Wenner and another coach break us up.

"Where's Maggie?" I ask.

Wenner looks at me like I've lost it. "At the nurse."

"I've got to see her."

"The only thing you're seeing is the principal's office, Becker. What's *wrong* with you?"

I'm escorted to Meyer's office. I have no choice since Wenner has my wrists pinned behind my back. "Wait here for Mr. Meyer," the coach orders.

But as soon as he leaves the office, I hop over the front desk and open the nurse's door. Maggie's pants are rolled up just above her knees.

My gaze immediately focuses on her scars.

The angry lines from where the doctors must have

sewed her up are pink and look like her leg has been clawed by a fierce animal.

By her knee, where the biggest sets of marks are, I think is a skin graft, because it's a darker shade and doesn't match the rest of her soft, ivory skin.

Tearing my gaze away from her leg, I look up at her. "I'm so sorry, Maggie," I say.

Her expression is hard, her eyes shuttered. "Go away, Caleb. Or do you want to take a picture so you could show Kendra? Then you'd both have something else to laugh about."

FORTY

Maggie

Caleb doesn't even know Mrs. Reynolds died. When I saw him in the hall this morning, I was going to tell him. But then I caught Caleb and Kendra together. Before our relationship started, I could understand. But I thought he liked me enough not to need someone else. I thought what we had was real. Ugh. I don't want to think about Kendra Greene and her perfect blonde hair and her perfect, perky boobs or the perfect way she walks.

But I can't help it.

Because I'm not perfect.

I'm sitting in the nurse's office to prove it. Ever since Caleb stood there frozen, gawking at the scars on my leg, I've been dying to get out of here. "Can I go back to class now?"

The school nurse is bent over my leg with rubber gloves, examining it. She looks up. "Does it hurt?"

You mean my heart? "No. It's fine," I say. "Really."

"There's a little blood here. I'm concerned there might be internal damage."

"It's just a little scratch," I say as the woman is putting antiseptic on a cotton ball and rubbing blood off my knee. "A big deal was made for nothing."

I know why Caleb came running over to me and acted all concerned. It's because he feels guilty that I overheard details about his relationship with Kendra. Drew was only telling the truth, that I was responsible for putting him in jail. Caleb and I should never have started talking. We should have kept ignoring each other at Mrs. Reynolds' house.

Because if we didn't talk, I wouldn't be so connected to him.

If we didn't talk, I wouldn't have kissed him and wanted more. I wouldn't have let him manipulate me.

Nurse Sandusky doesn't look happy as I get down off of the examining table and carefully lower my pant leg. But I'm not going to sit here and sulk all day. I'm going to get up and stand tall—to Caleb, to Drew, to Kendra . . . and whoever else decides to get in my way.

When I'm dressed, I breathe a sigh of relief. My scars are covered. So why do I feel so exposed? Because Caleb has seen the scars from the injuries he put on my body.

The forever scars that will make me think of him and the accident every day of my life.

Unfortunately I have to pass Meyer's office on my way out. Caleb is sitting in front of the secretary's desk, his head slumped in his hands.

As if he knows I'm watching him, he lifts his head up. His eyes bore into me as if they're seeking warmth or connection. Does he think I'm a fool who wants to be humiliated? I look away, wait for the nurse to write me a pass, and leave the office as fast as I can.

As if the day couldn't get worse, Kendra and Hannah are walking down the hall. They haven't seen me yet. I duck into the girls' bathroom . . . I've had enough for one day.

I look at myself in the bathroom mirror. Dull hazel eyes, hair that hasn't decided if it wants to be dark or light, and a nose that's too big for my face. On top of all those flaws, I have a limp.

How could I ever have thought I could compete with perfect Kendra Greene?

The bathroom door creaks open. I hide in one of the stalls and soon enough I hear Kendra say, "I can't imagine the two of them kissing. Can you?"

"Puh-leaze, Kend, don't gross me out. Caleb is, like, Hollywood tough guy and Maggie is, like, a total dork. She probably kisses with her lips all pursed and her hands at her sides."

"*Exactly*. You should have seen her this morning. I

thought she was going to cry right in the middle of the hall."

The two of them laugh.

I want to die. Forget standing tall, deep down I really am a dork and a coward.

I peek through the door opening. Hannah is putting on her lipstick while Kendra is playing with her big, blonde hair.

"He's always going to love you. You two have a bond that can't be broken," Hannah says.

Kendra stops playing with her hair and leans against one of the sinks. "Caleb told Brian he was interested in Maggie to throw him off."

"Why Maggie? Isn't she the least likely person to snag him? He *did* hit her with his car, you know. And she milks it for all it's worth."

Kendra hesitates.

"What?" Hannah asks.

"Did you check under the stalls?"

Oops. I'm dead meat. Balancing on top of the toilet seat with a bum leg is not an option.

The door to one of the stalls creaks open. Oh, no. I'm trying to peek through the door, but I don't want to stumble or make any sounds to alert them I'm spying.

"You two are so pathetic. You should have looked before you started babbling about your pathetic lives."

It's Sabrina, my cousin.

"What did you hear?" Kendra says.

"What do you think? I heard all of it."

"And you'll keep it to yourself, won't you Sabrina?"

Sabrina puts her hands on her hips. "I don't know. Why don't you stop spreading rumors about my cousin? She may limp, but she's got more to admire than both of you put together."

The other girls stare at Sabrina as if she sprouted wings, totally shocked that the follower finally proved she has a mind of her own.

"Get a grip, Sabrina. Don't forget, you were a loser and Maggie was in your spot a year ago. Just because you're friends with Brianne and Danielle now doesn't mean you're suddenly hot shit."

She's right. I wasn't nice to Sabrina when I was on top and she was struggling to keep friends that didn't hide in the library during lunch. I think Kendra's words are going to bring Sabrina down a notch, but my cousin doesn't miss a beat.

"Kendra, I used to worship the ground you walked on because you were pretty and popular and had a boyfriend the rest of the girls only dreamed they could get. I wanted to be popular, to be like you. Now I just think you're pathetic."

"You'd better watch yourself, Sabrina, or you might just find yourself a loser again so quick your head will spin." Kendra's eyes are wide and wild, and I think if she had superpowers they'd melt Sabrina with that one stare. But she doesn't have superpowers. Hannah is standing behind Kendra with her thumb and forefinger in an "L" on her forehead, directing it toward Sabrina.

While Sabrina is sticking up for me and being threatened, I'm hiding out like a coward. My palms are sweaty. I realize it's my own fear holding me back. I watch my cousin sticking up for me knowing the end result is not going to be pretty. I feel Mrs. Reynolds' spirit giving me courage.

I push the stall door open wide, the loud creak alerting all three to my presence.

Sabrina's face is as shocked as Kendra's and Hannah's.

Kendra gives a nervous laugh, but recovers quickly. "Is this, like, the designated loser bathroom and I never got the memo?"

"You're just like your cousin," Hannah says to me. "One who'll always follow in the footsteps of girls like me and Kendra."

I hobble next to my cousin. "Hannah, you and Kendra have it all. And yet . . . you're *both* empty shells, nothing worthwhile on the inside. I wouldn't follow you even if it meant healing my legs."

"I think the accident damaged your brain." Kendra spits out the words like a dragon would spit fire at its enemy.

Sabrina is watching me in shock. I know I haven't been strong since the accident. I never stick up for myself and I focus on my flaws instead of my assets. Spending time with a strong woman like Mrs. Reynolds must have rubbed off on me. And spending time with Caleb the past few months has made me feel attractive and beautiful. I just . . . deep down I can't believe he was lying to me. Admiration shined through the depths of his eyes. His fingers trembled when he traced my lips or touched my face. A guy like Caleb, who hides his emotions, couldn't fake those intense reactions even if he wanted to.

Kendra shakes her head and sneers at me. "If Caleb gave you any attention, he just felt sorry for you."

I'm sure he did . . . but what we shared went way beyond that. "I wouldn't sneer if I were you," I say to Kendra. "It doesn't suit your face."

My cousin turns to me. "Caleb? No, it can't be true. Can it?"

I nod.

"*The* Caleb Becker? Leah Becker's brother, Caleb Becker?"

I cock my head to the side and nod some more.

Sabrina's mouth drops open and her eyes bug out.

Like a shock wave, I realize Caleb had been right all along. Going to Spain was just a copout, a way to escape people and a way for me to forget the accident for a little while. But the accident happened. There is no way to forget it. And I limp. I have to face the fact I will never be the same as before.

It's okay. I'm okay. Taking a deep breath, I realize something . . .

I feel stronger and more alive than I did before the accident.

The door to the bathroom opens. Mrs. Gibbons walks

into the bathroom. Her eyebrows go up when she witnesses our little confrontation. "Aren't you all supposed to be in class?"

None of us answer. Kendra is staring at me, Hannah keeps looking from Kendra to me and back to Kendra, Sabrina still has her mouth open in shock, and I'm not revealing anything.

"Okay, then. Let's all take a little trip to Mr. Meyer's office so he can get to the bottom of this."

"Fine with me," I say.

"Me, too," Sabrina says, backing me up. I owe a big apology to her for being such a jerk before the accident. Sometimes you have to steer away from the crowd in order to be a better person. It's not always easy, that's for sure. But it's right. And sometimes doing the right thing feels so good. Even if it does end up in a trip to the principal's office.

Kendra's eyes are still spitting fire. "What*ever*."

"Yeah, what*ever*," Hannah says, doing an embarrassing imitation of her best friend. I almost feel sorry for her.

We all follow Mrs. Gibbons to the front office. Sabrina is looking at me, wide-eyed. "No way! Caleb Becker?" she mouths silently.

It's not Kendra's fault she's beautiful and pretty. It's not even Caleb's fault for being attracted to her. It doesn't even matter.

What matters is that I'm not carrying around feelings of hatred and betrayal. It's been too exhausting. Mrs. Reynolds was right.

I don't hate Kendra.

I don't hate Leah.

I don't hate Caleb.

I'm feeling stronger than I have in . . . well, I can't even remember when. All I know is that I feel good. No, better than that. I feel strong.

FORTY—ONE

Caleb

Meyer points to me and jabs his finger into the air with each word as he says, "Okay, Becker. In my office."

I follow him into his office, then he closes the door once I'm sitting in the chair opposite his desk. He's pissed off. I can tell by the way his neck muscles twitch and the colors of his face and bald head turn a deep shade of red. He doesn't even sit in his chair. He sits on the edge of his desk right over me. He's trying to be intimidating, to scare me into being a good kid. But he's never roomed with a guy like Julio. And if Julio didn't intimidate me, Meyer doesn't stand a chance.

"Why did you start a fight with Drew Rudolph?"

I can't tell him the truth. If the whole thing comes out,

Leah could be dragged into this, too. And Kendra. And Maggie. Leah has been acting creepy. I don't know what she'll end up saying. Will she blurt out the truth, that she was the one who hit Maggie? "I don't know," I say dumbly.

Meyer's anger deflates while frustration takes its place. "What *am* I going to do with you, Becker? I've had a parent call and say you were responsible for coercing a peer into consuming alcohol. Another complaint was filed by the wrestling coach from Fremont . . . something about you bullying one of his top wrestlers. You're on thin ice here, on the fast track to being a delinquent forever. Don't you understand the only person your behavior ultimately hurts is you? Unless you can explain yourself, I have no choice but to give you a suspension."

Suspension? Oh, shit. I would defend myself, but it's no use. The guy wouldn't believe me, anyway. I stay silent.

"You have nothing to say about these accusations?"

"Nope."

"Caleb, have a seat outside while I figure out how to proceed with this."

So now I'm stuck in another metal chair outside Meyer's office. Closed doors and metal chairs are the recurring themes in my life.

I look up when the door to the front office opens.

Maggie walks in the office, just feet from where I'm sitting. Only able to check her out from the side, I study her face. She has high cheekbones and a straight nose. It's not small; it has a little bump in the middle, almost as if

God wanted to put it there so her nose wouldn't be perfect. She wouldn't be Maggie without that imperfection. She's not in-your-face pretty like Kendra, but there's something about her . . . that mix of insecurity and regal features that don't fit. Every one of her features reflects who she is. Except her scars.

Those I wish I could take away with a touch of my fingers and transfer them to my own body.

Maggie is focused on the counter, reading something intently. Her hair falls like a curtain shielding her face from me. I'm barely aware of Sabrina, Kendra, and Hannah in the room, too. This place is getting crowded.

Mrs. Gibbons, the art teacher, knocks on Meyer's door. She peeks her head inside when he barks for her to enter his sacred domain. "We've had a situation with some of the senior girls."

The girls head single file into his office. Kendra looks defiant, Hannah looks scared, Sabrina looks indifferent, and Maggie is . . . she seems resolved to handle whatever comes flying at her.

The girls come out a few minutes later. Maggie doesn't look at me. She files out of the office with the rest of the girls.

Meyer reappears at the door. "Okay, Becker. Your turn."

I go into his office and am directed to yet another chair. This one is padded. I rest my elbows on my knees and think of what Meyer said: I'm on the fast track for being a delinquent forever. Maggie was probably right: if you disappear, then you don't have to always be reminded of the past wherever you turn.

I did my community service, but haven't gotten my final release papers. Damon is seriously going to kill me when he finds out I got in a fight. What the hell is going to happen when I go back to the DOC? I hope Mom and Leah don't go over the edge.

I hear the clicking of shoes and look up. My mother is standing in the doorway of Meyer's office. Her lips are tight. I can sense she has a loose rein on control because I see her wobbling slightly from side to side.

"Ah, Mrs. Becker," Meyer says. "Thanks for coming so quickly."

Mom nods and holds onto the door frame. "So . . . should I take him home?"

Meyer walks up to my mom and puts his hand on her shoulder to steady her. "The boy whom Caleb assaulted has not filed any charges as yet, but policy forces me to keep him off school grounds until this is resolved. You'll get a call from me after I've consulted the district superintendent to inform you of the length of Caleb's suspension."

Mom nods, then focuses on me. She looks tired. The deep lines under her eyes and at the corners of her mouth look deeper than I've ever seen them. I put those lines there. Without meaning to, I've broken my mother's spirit.

In the car, I've got nothing to say. And when silent tears start dripping out of her tired eyes, all I want to do is escape. Because I can't tell her anything to make her feel better, I can't fight this snowball of bullshit that has become my life.

I sit in my room until darkness falls, when someone knocks on my door. "Caleb, open up," a familiar transition counselor's voice rings out.

Great, now I get to be reamed out by Damon.

"Let me have it," I say dryly as I let him in.

If you've never seen a black guy's face get red with anger, you've never seen Damon Manning pissed off. "What the hell is going on? I got a call from your principal this afternoon telling me you're suspended for two weeks. You want to go back to the DOC?"

"Sure. You got cuffs ready?" I say, holding my arms out in front of me.

Damon gets in my face, real close. "Listen, punk, I have no problem slapping cuffs on you and hauling your ass back to prison. But I don't think you realize your eighteenth birthday is just around the corner. And you know what kind of eighteenth birthday present you get from the State of Illinois? You get transferred to the big boy jail. That's right, the adult place where the inmates rule, and not one day will go by that you won't be threatened or forced to do shit you've only heard about. I don't want you in there, Caleb, because you'll go in a confused smartass boy and come out a hardened bastard. They'll eat you alive there and nobody can save your ass. You hear me? Now tell me why the hell you've been getting into fights."

I'm so used to pleading guilty, I forget sometimes to

tell the truth. I look Damon straight on, no playing around this time. "I was protecting Maggie. Drew insulted her."

Damon takes my desk chair and sits in it. He puts his hand on his forehead and starts rubbing it, kind of like Meyer did this afternoon. "Caleb, what're you doing? She's your *victim*. You hit her with your car."

"I didn't do it."

"What?" he snaps.

"I said I didn't mean to do it."

Damon takes his hand off his forehead and leans forward. "I don't know what you're trying to pull here, but it's not good. If you can't pretend Maggie doesn't exist, then leave town. She called my boss this morning expressing concern about her safety. She said you've been sexual with her, and now that it's over you've harassed her."

"What?"

Damon looks straight at me. "Maggie Armstrong says she's filing a complaint. Oh, don't look so shocked, Caleb. What did you expect? When you don't follow the rules you pay the consequences. It's simple."

Nothing is that simple. I swallow. My throat feels constricted. Maggie hates me enough to send me back to the DOC?

"I need to know," Damon continues. "Did you have a sexual encounter with her?"

I sit on my bed and rest my head in my hands. Jeez, this cannot be happening. "That depends on what you mean by a sexual encounter."

"Don't fuck with me, Becker."

"I *didn't* have sex with her."

"Did you harass her?"

I shake my head. "We had a relationship, a *mutual* relationship. It was no big deal. It's over. Done."

"How did it end?"

"Abruptly."

Damon blows out a breath in frustration, then pulls out a stack of papers from his briefcase. "I got your release papers signed. You finished your community service."

I stare at the papers as if they have angels' wings on them, but my head is still reeling. I thought what Maggie and I shared was . . . well, it was a hell of a lot more than I ever had with Kendra. If Maggie hooked up with me just for revenge . . . oh, hell.

"You're released, but we have a bit of a problem. You can't go back to school. Caleb?"

"Yeah."

"Everybody isn't against you, you know."

I nod. Right now, I can't agree. I was so pumped to fix everything when I returned home. But all I've been doing is fighting instead of fixing. I'm at a loss here.

After Damon leaves, I head to the kitchen. Mom is leaning against the sink. She's shaking as she takes a bunch of pills and swallows them with a gulp of water.

"Mom, what are you doing?"

"Taking medication for tension and stress."

I snatch the bottle of pills off the counter.

"Give me that back," she orders.

Taking a closer look at the drug's name on the bottle. Diazepam. Valium. "How long have you been taking these?"

"Give them back," she says, pulling the bottle from my hand and clutching them as if they hold her sanity.

"You can overdose on that shit, Mom. It's dangerous."

My mom laughs, a throaty laugh so strong it makes her cough.

"Is that why you've been avoiding getting close to me. You've become a closet pill popper?" Damn, why didn't I see this before?

"It's not in the closet anymore, is it?"

"Does Dad know?"

"What do you think? It's the only way I can keep a smile on my face all day. He doesn't like to think about the bad stuff. He's too busy. I've been a failure, haven't I? A terrible wife, a terrible mother . . . it's no wonder I was kicked out of the Ladies' Auxiliary."

"Stop caring what everyone thinks!" I yell. "You're killing the entire family."

"Did you think about *the entire family* when you hit Maggie?" she whispers, then huffs out a disgusted breath.

"This isn't about me, Mom." I don't tell her it never was about me.

She shakes her head. "You don't get it, Caleb, do you? There's four people living in this house and we're all strangers. It *is* about you. It's about all of us."

I don't even know who I am anymore. I thought I did, but with Maggie's betrayal I'm back where I started.

My mom turns to face the sink, her body shaking and wrought with despair. As I walk over and put my arms around her, I want to tell her I'll help her. I need help, too. But she stiffens as soon as I make contact. "Don't touch me."

I take my hands off her and back away. Everything around me is crashing into a million pieces. There's no way I can mend them no matter how hard I try. "Don't wait up," I grind out before leaving the kitchen and taking the stairs two steps at a time. I bang on Leah's bedroom door. "Open up."

"What do you want?" Leah says through the door.

I pound harder. "Leah, open this door or I'll break it down."

She opens it right before I'm about to kick it open. "What?"

"How long has Mom been abusing prescription drugs?"

She shrugs. "After you got sentenced. She stopped for a while, but started up again when you got released."

"How can you just stand there like it's no big deal?"

Leah stares at me and cocks her head to the side, her black makeup in stark contrast to her white skin, making her look like a mime. "When she's numb she doesn't ask questions."

Huh? I stare at my sister as if she's a ghost, a shell of a person I once knew. "Do you even have a conscience anymore?"

Leah shrugs.

I grab her shoulders and yell, "Leah, grow up and finally take responsibility for something . . . anything!"

Tears start streaming down her cheeks. I shouldn't be satisfied that I'm making my sister cry, but I swear any emotion from her pleases me. I feel her emotions, too. But they're so conflicted with mine I can't be close to her. Not now. A part of Leah has always been a part of me. Her misery has become mine, and right now I want nothing to do with it.

She's sobbing while I leave the house and head down the street.

I walk ten houses away before I realize where I'm headed: Mrs. Reynolds' house. The lady is the only one who's tough enough to help. Maybe she'll let me live with her, in that little room above the garage.

Waiting twenty minutes for a bus to come to take me to Hampton seems like forever. When it comes and I take one look at the old lady's house, I feel like I'm home.

I ring the doorbell, hoping she can hear it. Maybe I'll install one of those bulbs that light up every time the doorbell rings, so if her hearing really goes she'll be all set.

The second time I ring, the door opens. But it's not Mrs. Reynolds, it's the guy who owns Auntie Mae's Diner. "Is Mrs. Reynolds home?"

"Aren't you Caleb Becker?"

"Yeah. I—"

"How do you know my mother?" he demands.

I put my hands in my pockets. "I worked for her."

He hesitates, confused, then his mouth goes wide. "*You* built the gazebo?"

"Yeah."

"While Maggie Armstrong worked here? The both of you, together?"

"With Mrs. Reynolds," I assure him.

"Did she know you were the one that hit Maggie? Forget it, from the look on your face I assume my mother knew. She probably tried to patch everything up, didn't she?"

"Yes, sir. I need to talk to Mrs. Reynolds." She's the only one I have left now.

"She passed away yesterday morning."

No. No, this can't happen. A hole forms in my chest and spreads through my veins. "You're lying."

"My mother had a heart attack in her sleep. Now I don't know what's been going on here, but I know Maggie's mother doesn't want you hanging around her daughter. Respect the family and leave her be."

"No problem. No problem at all," I say.

FORTY-TWO

Maggie

Mom told me Mr. Reynolds had a surprise for me. I went to Auntie Mae's Diner after school and Mr. Reynolds gave me the keys to his mom's Cadillac. I protested, but Mom assured me Mrs. Reynolds would want me to have it.

So now Mom is driving me to Mrs. Reynolds' house on her break. She helps me open the garage. I smile when I see the car, remembering the time Mrs. Reynolds helped me get over my fear of driving.

"You sure you're ready to do this?" Mom asks.

"Yeah, I'm sure. Now get back to work. I'll be fine."

"Maggie, you've been so strong lately, but I don't know if you're ready for this."

It's time I tell her how I'm feeling. I've been trying to hold it in so I don't hurt her, when all along I think I'll hurt her more if I don't say anything. "Mom, I need some space," I say, then gauge her reaction. She's looking at me skeptically, but I can tell by the way her lips are together in concentration that she's listening and attempting to understand.

I take a deep breath and say, "I know it's hard for you. It's been unbelievably difficult for me . . . but I'm finally ready to accept my body and my limitations. I'm me . . . the new me. It might not be a perfect me, but I'm okay with that. It's about time I stopped trying to escape my life, don't you think?"

A tear runs down my mom's cheek. She smiles at me, this warm smile that reaches her eyes. "The accident . . . it took a part of you away."

"Only because I let it."

Now we're both crying. I give her a long hug.

After a few minutes she gets in her car and drives away from the house, giving me the space I need. Taking a deep breath, I scan the yard. And swallow hard. The gazebo is standing like a castle in the middle of the grass, outlined by the flower beds. The bulbs are patiently waiting in hibernation until it's their time to poke their heads out of the ground for the first time and vibrantly come to life.

After yesterday, I feel like I've bloomed. It took a romance and an old lady to coax me out of hibernation, but it happened.

As I'm carefully driving home, I see Caleb at Paradise

Park at the basketball courts. I stop to let him know I'm not upset he betrayed me. I'll get over him. It might take a while, but I'm going to be just fine. I'll have other boyfriends and adventures in life, other times I'll be able to feel confident and carefree and happy. I'm a survivor. Even with my limp. Getting out of the car and gathering all my courage, I walk over to him.

He sees me, but doesn't stop dribbling the ball.

"Caleb," I call out.

"Why didn't you tell me about Mrs. Reynolds?"

"I didn't have a chance. I wanted to," I say, then step toward him.

"You better stay back or I might start harassing you."

Okay, I deserve that. I did slap him and refuse his help yesterday. But that was before I straightened everything out in my head. "I heard you got in trouble."

"You come here to rub it in or you want to challenge me to a one-on-one?" he says.

"You know I can't play."

He looks me up and down suggestively. "Oh, you play, Maggie. Maybe not basketball, your games are more complicated than that."

"What are you talking about?"

He takes the basketball and holds it at his side, then gives a short laugh. "I can't believe you're afraid of me."

I move forward, stepping closer to him and putting my chin in the air with confidence. "I'm not afraid of you."

He stands before me with as much confidence as I'm showing him. "Prove it."

"How?"

He tosses the basketball to the side of the court and steps toward me, closing the distance between us. "Figure it out."

My breath catches and I panic. "I . . . I don't know what you mean."

"I think you do," he says, coming so close I can almost feel his emotions as my own.

"You want me to kiss you?" I ask breathlessly.

"You've ruined me, you do know that don't you?" he says right before I stand on my tiptoes and touch my lips to his.

He grabs my waist and pulls me close so I can feel the full strength and length of his body against mine. My fingers wrap around his biceps at the same time. I'm lost in the protection of his embrace and the smell and taste that's uniquely Caleb Becker. Uniquely . . . us.

As our kiss turns more intense, I sense a change in him. He's kissing harder, fuller. Angry.

I stumble backwards and push him away from me. "What are you doing?"

He wipes his mouth with the back of his hand. "Making sure I scare you. It's what you want, isn't it? So you can claim being the victim."

We're standing here staring at each other. Controller and controlled. Perpetrator and victim. Boy and girl.

He picks up his basketball. "Go home, Maggie. You got what you came for."

Movement out of the corner of my eye catches my attention, breaking the connection. It's Leah.

"Caleb, Mom and Dad want you home. Now," she says.

I smooth down my hair, pat dirt off my pants, clear my throat, and do everything but look at the two of them.

Then I run back to the car as fast as I can.

FORTY-THREE
Caleb

"You didn't tell her that I hit her, did you?" Leah asks as she watches Maggie run away from the park.

I shake my head.

"But you and Maggie. I saw how you looked at her and I knew . . ."

"What?" I say quickly, then look my sister straight in the eye.

I start walking back home and my sister steps in beside me. "Getting mixed up with Maggie can ruin our family, Caleb."

"Lay off, Leah. I mean it." I turn to her. "I've just about had it."

When I get home, my parents are waiting for me by

the front door. My dad is standing rigid, a stern look on his face. My mom is beside him. I can tell she's totally out of it.

"Where were you last night?" Dad orders in such a stern voice you'd think I was out committing murder.

"Visiting an old friend. What's the big deal?"

My mom looks at my dad.

I hold my arms wide. "What?"

"I saw Maggie coming from the direction of the park," Dad says.

"So? It's a free country, Dad. People can walk where they want to."

My mom clutches her arms tight, grabbing on to her sweater. "We just don't want to see you get into trouble. People talk . . ."

"About what?"

"I don't want to discuss it," Mom says, then starts to walk woodenly back into the house, no doubt to numb herself again.

"Let's hash it out. Right here, right now."

"Caleb, please, not so loud." My mom glances nervously at the neighbors' houses, making sure they don't witness the scene I'm about to make. God, I wish she'd stop worrying about appearances and see that her family is falling apart.

"What are people saying?"

"Nothing, Caleb. Everything's fine. Now stop this nonsense."

I step into the middle of the front yard and say as loud as I can, "Are they saying I've been starting fights at school? Are they saying I'm harassing Maggie? Making my friends drink alcohol? You think it's true, don't you? Come on, hit me with the fucking gossip already!"

"Now you've crossed the line," Dad says, stepping between us. "Go inside the house and calm down. You can apologize to your mother before supper."

I snap, like a rubber band that'd been pulled so tight for so long it just breaks apart violently. Kissing Maggie, school suspension, Kendra's manipulations, my sister's warning, my parents' inability to face reality, my mom's addiction problem, the false gossip . . . all of it is driving me nuts.

"I'm not leaving this spot until we have it all out on the table," I say. I look at my sister.

"Caleb!" Leah cries. "Please stop."

My dad's posture stiffens even more, his lips purse and the expression in his eyes is hard. "This is my home," he says. "And as long as you live here you'll abide by my rules. Now go inside the house, leave your mother in peace, and . . . calm . . . down!"

I swallow, hard. It's not easy for me to say the next words coming from my mouth, but I can't hold it in any longer. My family is screwed up, each and every one of us. They want to stay ignorant, to forget reality and live in a made-up world they've created. It's fake, it's sick . . . and I can't do it. I think the only way they'll heal is if I'm not here. I'm the root of their problems. If I take the root away, I'll remove the problem.

"I'm leaving," I say.

My thoughts turn to Maggie, the one girl who I used to think wasn't worth a second glance. But when it comes right down to it, she's the strongest girl I know. She confronted me about Kendra before the accident, she goes to school even though people laugh at the way she moves, and she worked her ass off for Mrs. Reynolds in order to achieve her dream of going to Spain. The accident made her a stronger person. Hell, she made *me* a stronger person.

"Where do you think you're going?" Dad demands.

"Inside to pack, then I'm out of here. I can't live with shame and denial around me. And you shouldn't, either."

"This is who we are now, son. The accident changed us . . . all of us. We were fine until you messed it all up."

I shake my head. "Don't you want to go back to the way it was before? I would do anything to make this family normal again."

"Shouldn't you have thought of that before you hit Maggie? I would have never thought I'd say this to my own son, but you . . . Caleb Becker . . . are a selfish bastard."

I walk past my parents and Leah, heading to my room. Pulling a duffle bag out of my closet, I stuff it without really thinking. I'm ready in five minutes, then look back at my room one last time.

My lightsaber is still on my shelf, waiting for me until I return. But I'm not coming back. Hopefully, after I leave, my mom won't have to drug her life to make it bearable and Leah can live her life the way she wants—with or without the truth. And Dad . . . well, one day he'll have to face reality. When he's ready.

It's up to me now to pave the way for myself and to stop trying to make sure life is back to normal. Screw normal. Normal doesn't exist. Caleb Becker's family doesn't exist. I'm on my own now.

With a sigh of determination I step back in the room, snatch the lightsaber, shove it in the duffle, and head out. Leah is at the front door, blocking it. "Don't leave," she begs.

"Get out of my way."

"Mom and Dad need you, Caleb. I need you."

I give a short laugh. "Mom and Dad'll be just fine. They like living in denial. As for you . . ." I take in her black attire. "You've got to get past the accident. Face the facts before people like Kendra make you face them. I can't protect you anymore. It's time to protect yourself."

I move around her and walk outside. I have no clue where I'm going or what to do, but I feel free. Tossing my duffle over my shoulder, I start walking. When I reach Maggie's house, I don't see her but I know she's inside.

I give her a goodbye salute and keep walking.

Mrs. Reynolds' gazebo is where I spend the cold, lonely night. When a shooting star flies above me as I stare up at the sky, I wonder if it's the old lady giving me a sign.

FORTY-FOUR

Maggie

Caleb kissed me last night at the basketball courts. I kissed him back. I still can't believe either of those things happened. I thought I was okay without needing him so much. I should have wiped off my lips and washed them with soap before I'd gone to bed, but instead I kept looking in the mirror. My lips are still puffy, a reminder of how Caleb's own lips were hot and demanding.

For years I'd imagined what kissing Caleb would feel like and taste like. To be honest, I wanted to push him away, to make him want me like I wanted him and to reject him like he rejected me.

But I couldn't.

All those feelings from my childhood came back, from the time Caleb urged me down from the tree in front of my house to the time he took the blame for that broken statue. I can't even forget the times he patted my back while I was crying to Leah about my parents' divorce. For the past year, the accident ruled my life and molded me into who I've become.

I've taken back my life.

Sitting on my bed, I pull up my pant leg. I notice that my heart is racing a little less as I scan the scars with my eyes. I used to think of them as angry scars, but now I don't see them as angry. They aren't even scary. I trace the lines with my fingers, and I don't even wish they'd disappear. They're a part of me.

I close my eyes, remembering the accident. It's so strange to think about that night without massive emotions running rampant through my veins. Through the darkness behind my lids, the image of Caleb driving the car that hit me is outlined in my head. But something doesn't feel right.

Chills run up and down my spine.

Because, as I shut my eyes tight, the image of the driver becomes clearer and the foggy haze dissipates.

It's Leah. A look of horror and fear in her eyes as she loses control of the car.

Leah was the one who hit me that night.

Not Caleb.

Why would he . . . why would they . . . ?

The doorbell rings while I'm still trying to sort it all out. My stomach is queasy. I want to throw up. But I can't, because my mother is calling me downstairs. I almost fall down as I greet a man and a woman wearing matching dark navy suits.

"Maggie, we're from the Illinois Juvenile Department of Corrections. We're here to investigate your complaint about Caleb Becker."

"I didn't file a complaint," I tell them.

The woman opens her briefcase and pulls out a folder. "We have documentation you called the 1-800 juvenile justice number complaining to the operator that Caleb Becker was harassing you."

Oh my God. I shake my head and look to my mom. "I didn't call. Mom, I swear I didn't call."

"Are you sure?" the man asks. "You don't have to be afraid, Maggie. We're here to make sure you're protected."

I stand up. "I'm not afraid of Caleb. We're friends."

My mom says, "Please excuse my daughter. She doesn't know what she's talking about. She's been instructed not to have any contact with that boy. Right, Maggie?"

I bite down on my bottom lip. "Mom . . ."

"Maggie?"

Last night at the park makes sense now, why he was testing me. Oh, how he must hate me, thinking I'd call and complain when I would never do anything to hurt him. Kendra would hurt him. I wouldn't. "I have to go see him."

"Maggie, come back here!"

I hobble over to the Beckers' house before anyone can stop me. Mrs. Becker answers the door.

"Is Caleb home?" I ask frantically. "I really, really need to talk to him. I know you probably hate me for being the reason he went to jail, but I think it was all a mistake and—"

"Caleb is gone," she says, totally unfazed by the words coming from her mouth. She even has a strange smile on her face. "He left."

By now my mom has followed me over to the Beckers' house with the investigators in tow.

Mom regards Mrs. Becker strangely. "Penny, what's wrong with you?"

As soon as my mom says it, Mrs. Becker slips and falls right into my mom's arms. After Mom shrieks, the two investigators help her carry Mrs. Becker into the house. "She's passed out," one of them says.

As they're taking care of Mrs. Becker, I step back. What did Mrs. Becker mean when she said Caleb *has gone?* I rush home, grab my keys and drive to Mrs. Reynolds' house. I check the garage, gazebo . . . he's not here.

All along, I blamed Caleb for hitting me, without questioning his guilt. He pleaded guilty, but deep down I detected something strange in him. I thought it was a lack of remorse for hitting me, when all along it was a lack of guilt.

My heart sinks lower with each passing moment as I drive around Paradise. I'm looking for Caleb, or some sign he's still here. Before I know it, I'm at the place where my life changed.

The scene of the accident.

The skid marks from the car are still on the curb, a dark reminder of that day. I haven't come here since the accident. I wouldn't have had the strength before to relive it up close. I step out of the car and walk over to the fading skid marks, staring at them for what seems like forever. Will they eventually disappear altogether, so the only physical reminders of the accident will be the ones I carry with me?

I know the truth, though. That the visible scars aren't as deep as the emotional ones Leah and Caleb have been struggling with. I have a burning desire to help them, just as Caleb helped me. The most important thing I've learned the past few months is that friends are invaluable. People you love can get you through the toughest of times. They need me just as I need them. I miss Leah as my confidante, my best friend. And the love I have for Caleb is the forever kind that will never go away, no matter how hard I try to deny it.

"Maggie."

I turn around. Caleb is riding in a black Toyota, a guy I don't recognize at the wheel. Caleb tells the guy to stop the car, then he walks up to me. He looks sad and lonely and worried.

"How did we get here?" I ask.

"Here's where it all started."

"I didn't call and complain about you," I say hurriedly.

"You see, these investigators came to my house this morning and said they were following up on a complaint I made and I insisted I never made it and then I realized you must have thought I did and then—"

Caleb puts a finger to my lips, stopping my babble. "It doesn't matter."

"But it does. And I trust you. Isn't that what we're all about? Trust and honesty."

I need to prove it to him, a sign that I trust him without any reservations. I pull up my left pant leg with one hand, revealing all my scars up to my knee.

His brows knit together in pain, as if he was the one who put them on my leg. I take his hand in mine and together we trace the swollen lines with our fingers. "You see, there's nothing I want to hide from you anymore. Do you feel the same, Caleb? No secrets, no lies?" I need him to tell me the truth about what happened that night. I need to hear it from his own lips, his own words. *Tell me you didn't hit me*, I want to say. *Tell me the truth.*

"Yo, *amigo*, you ready to *vamónos?*" a guy yells from the car.

"Who is that?"

"Rio."

I'm worried. "I mean, who *is* he?"

"You don't want to know, Maggie," Caleb says. "Listen, I gotta go."

I look up into his beautiful, intense face. At the same time I know he's never going to give away the secret he's been holding inside. That fierce, protective spirit is a part of him, a bond he can't break.

"Where are you going? When will you be back?"

"I'm not coming back."

Looking into his serious, sad eyes, I know he means what he's saying. My eyes start to water and tears roll down my cheeks. "You can't leave me. Not now." I want to beg and plead and cry and grab him until he changes his mind. I want to play tennis with him today, and tomorrow, and the next day.

He gently swipes my tears with his fingers. "Then come with me."

The tables have cruelly turned. I tell him, "I realized you were right. It's a copout to leave. I'm going to stay in Paradise until I graduate, and save the money Mrs. Reynolds gave me for college."

"Becker, you comin' or not?" the guy in the car calls out.

Caleb nods and says, "Yeah, I'm coming."

I lean in and touch his forehead to mine. "Tell me what we had was real," I whisper. "Please."

Caleb's hands lightly clasp my head on both sides, enclosing us into our own private world. "As real as it gets. Don't ever question that, no matter what. Okay?"

"Right now I'm questioning everything. Why did I even come here?"

"Because you're ready to start a new life, Maggie. You're free of the past now. It can't hurt you. For me, being free means leaving Paradise." Leaning in, he kisses me. So soft and full of warmth and longing and remorse.

I want to grab him and keep him safe. "Does that mean we're both free?"

He nods, unable to put it into words.

I know he'll never write or call. He's going to cut all ties with his family and this little town that's caused him so much grief. Including me. God, how I wish Caleb never pled guilty to hitting me. Although if the accident had never happened, if he'd never gone to jail and been stuck doing community service, Caleb and I might never have been together.

I wouldn't have changed that for anything.

He steps back and winks at me. "Bye."

"I'm not going to say it back to you, you know," I tell him.

He gives a short laugh and keeps retreating backwards. "Then tell me something I can remember as your last words to me. Tell me you love me. Tell me you'll think of me every night before you sleep. Tell me—"

"*The red hen has flown the coop,*" I say.

He laughs. "I'll always remember Mrs. Reynolds, the gazebo, the daffodils, you and me in the gazebo . . ." Caleb winks at me one more time and turns around, his back to me as he walks to the Toyota. I want to scream at him for leaving me. I want to run up to him and forget being sane. Let us live in the streets together. As long as we're a team, nothing can bring us lower than we were apart.

But he never did tell me it was Leah who hit me. He's the one who, in the end, didn't trust me . . . or himself.

I'm sobbing now, more than I did after the accident. And my heart hurts, more pain oozing from it than my leg ever had.

"Caleb!" I yell right before he slides into the passenger seat and closes the car door. I hold my breath, waiting for him to come back to me. To turn around. But he doesn't.

The car screeches away, its red lights a blur through my watery eyes.

I head back home and some time during the ride I stop crying. There's strength within me that I didn't know existed before. It's as if Mrs. Reynolds is nudging me to stay strong. Life is too short, she'd once said. She was right. As I pull into my driveway and get out of my car, I notice Leah. She's standing in the front doorway of her house, her eyes puffy.

I walk over to her. "Is your mom okay?"

She shrugs. "I guess. Your mom's with her."

Well, it's a step in the right direction. It's about time we mended that invisible fence. I look up at my old best friend.

"You saw him, didn't you?" she asks me.

"Yeah."

She holds her arm over her eyes and starts to sob. "I need to tell you something really, really important. But I can't look at you while I do it."

I take her arm and lower it. "You don't have to tell me right now," I say. "When you're ready, we can talk."

"You're going to hate me, Maggie. For the rest of your life you're going to hate me."

"I'm not going to hate you. I know, Leah. I know what it is."

"You do?" she says, all glassy-eyed.

"Yeah. But it's okay."

"It is?"

"Let's just say our friendship means more to me than holding a grudge or living in the past. You know what always helps me forget?"

"What?"

"A pie run."

Leah gives me a small smile behind her tears. "You're kidding, right?"

"Nope. Come with me for a drive to Auntie Mae's. Let's get our moms . . . I think they need some pie, too."

About the Author

Simone was a teen in the 80s and still overuses words like "grody" and "totally," but resists the urge to wear blue eye shadow or say "gag me with a spoon." When Simone's not writing, she's speaking to high schools or teaching writing. In her spare time, she TiVos reality television and watches teen movies. She lives near Chicago with her family and two dogs.

Simone loves to hear from her readers! Visit her at www.simoneelkeles.com.

Maggie and Caleb's Story Continues...

The breathtaking sequel to **Leaving Paradise**

Coming Fall 2010